What Kids Say About Carole Marsh Mysteries . . .

I love the real locations! Reading the book always makes me want to go and visit them all on our next family vacation. My Mom says maybe, but I can't wait!

One day, I want to be a real kid in one of Ms. Marsh's mystery books. I think it would be fun, and I think I am a real character anyway. I filled out the application and sent it in and am keeping my fingers crossed!

History was not my favorite subject till I started reading Carole Marsh Mysteries. Ms. Marsh really brings history to life. Also, she leaves room for the scary and fun.

I think Christina is so smart and brave. She is lucky to be in the mystery books because she gets to go to a lot of places. I always wonder just how much of the book is true and what is made up. Trying to figure that out is fun!

Grant is cool and funny! He makes me laugh a lot!!

I like that there are boys and girls in the story of different ages. Some mysteries I outgrow, but I can always find a favorite character to identify with in these books.

They are scary, but not too scary. They are funny. I learn a lot. There is always food which makes me hungry. I feel like I am there.

What Adults Say About Carole Marsh Mysteries . . .

I think kids love these books because they have such a wealth of detail. I know I learn a lot reading them! It's an engaging way to look at the history of any place or event. I always say I'm only going to read one chapter to the kids, but that never happens–it's always two or three, at least! –Librarian

Reading the mystery and going on the field trip–Scavenger Hunt in hand–was the most fun our class ever had! It really brought the place and its history to life. They loved the real kids characters and all the humor. I loved seeing them learn that reading is an experience to enjoy! –4th grade teacher

Carole Marsh is really on to something with these unique mysteries. They are so clever; kids want to read them all. The Teacher's Guides are chock full of activities, recipes, and additional fascinating information. My kids thought I was an expert on the subject–and with this tool, I felt like it! –3rd grade teacher

My students loved writing their own Real Kids/Real Places mystery book! Ms. Marsh's reproducible guidelines are a real jewel. They learned about copyright and more & ended up with their own book they were so proud of! –Reading/Writing Teacher

The Mystery in the ROCKY MOUNTAINS

by

Carole Marsh

Second Printing April 2006

Published by Gallopade International/Carole Marsh Books. Printed in the United States of America.

Cover design: Vicki DeJoy; Editor: Chad Beard; Graphic Design: Steve St. Laurent; Layout and footer design: Lynette Rowe; Photography: Michael Boylan.

Gallopade is proud to be a member and supporter of these educational organizations and associations:

American Booksellers Association
American Library Association
International Reading Association
National Association for Gifted Children
The National School Supply and Equipment Association
The National Council for the Social Studies
Museum Store Association
Association of Partners for Public Lands

This book is dedicated to all the wonderful children who have been characters in my mystery books . . . and those who may be "real characters" in the future!

For additional information on Carole Marsh Mysteries, visit:
www.carolemarshmysteries.com

Reading up on the Rocky Mountains!

20 Years Ago . . .

As a mother and an author, one of the fondest periods of my life was when I decided to write mystery books for children. At this time (1979) kids were pretty much glued to the TV, something parents and teachers complained about the way they do about video games today.

I decided to set each mystery in a real place–a place kids could go and visit for themselves after reading the book. And I also used real children as characters. Usually a couple of my own children served as characters, and I had no trouble recruiting kids from the book's location to also be characters.

Also, I wanted all the kids–boys and girls of all ages–to participate in solving the mystery. And, I wanted kids to learn something as they read. Something about the history of the location. And I wanted the stories to be funny.

That formula of real+scary+smart+fun served me well. The kids and I had a great time visiting each site and many of the events in the stories actually came out of our experiences there. (For example, we really did spend the night in the Brown Palace Hotel, see a tuba concert, ride the Ski Train, fall off the ski chair lift, go to the Ski Ball, and have many more adventures in the snowy Rocky Mountains!)

I love getting letters from teachers and parents who say they read the book with their class or child, then visited the historic site and saw all the places in the mystery for themselves. What's so great about that? What's great is that you and your children have an experience that bonds you together forever. Something you shared. Something you both cared about at the time. Something that crossed all age levels–a good story, a good scare, a good laugh!

20 years later,

Carole Marsh

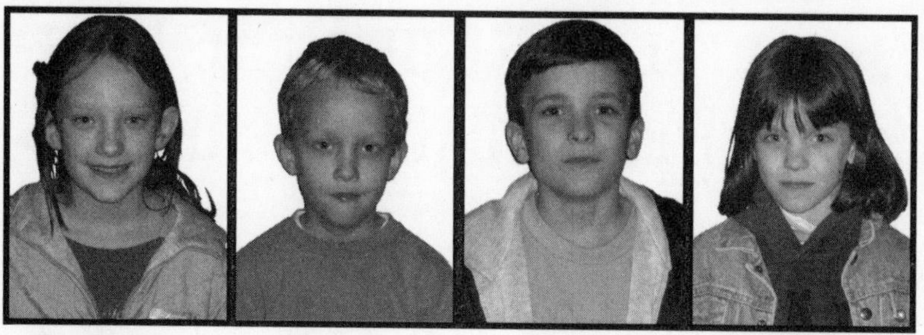

Christina Yother **Grant Yother** **Zander Yother** **Dakota Yother**

BOUT THE CHARACTERS

Christina Yother, 9, from Peachtree City, Georgia

Grant Yother, 7, from Peachtree City, Georgia
Christina's brother

Zander Yother, age 11, Grant's and Christina's real cousin, from Rome, Georgia, as Zander from Albuquerque, New Mexico and Salt Lake City, Utah

Dakota Yother, age 8, Zander's sister

The many places featured in the book actually exist and are worth a visit! Perhaps you could read the book and follow the trail these kids went on during their mysterious adventure!

Titles in the Real Kids Real Places Series

#1 The Mystery of Biltmore House

#2 The Mystery at the Boston Marathon

#3 The Mystery of Blackbeard the Pirate

#4 The Mystery of the Alamo Ghost

#5 The Mystery on the California Mission Trail

#6 The Mystery of the Missing Dinosaurs

#7 The White House Christmas Mystery

#8 The Mystery on Alaska's Iditarod Trail

#9 The Mystery at Kill Devil Hills

#10 The Mystery in New York City

#11 The Mystery at Disney World

#12 The Mystery on the Underground Railroad

#13 The Mystery in the Rocky Mountains

#14 The Mystery on the Mighty Mississippi

#15 The Mystery at the Kentucky Derby

#16 The Ghost of the Grand Canyon

CONTENTS

1 What a Pointy Airport!

"Let's see," said Christina, with a big yawn. "I looked out the window over Georgia, Tennessee, and Missouri. I ate over Kansas. And I slept over . . . well, I guess I don't know what I slept over, but isn't it time to BE THERE?" She squirmed beneath her snug seatbelt.

Her grandmother, Mimi, gently rubbed the top of Christina's soft, brown hair. "I know it's been a long ride," she agreed.

"But we've begun our descent and are just about to come in for our landing," Christina's grandfather, Papa, told her. Papa had his own pilot's license and his own cute, little red airplane, so he knew a lot about aviation stuff.

Christina shook her younger brother, Grant. "Wake up! Wake up!" she warned him. "We're coming down!"

Grant sat up with a start. His naturally curly hair

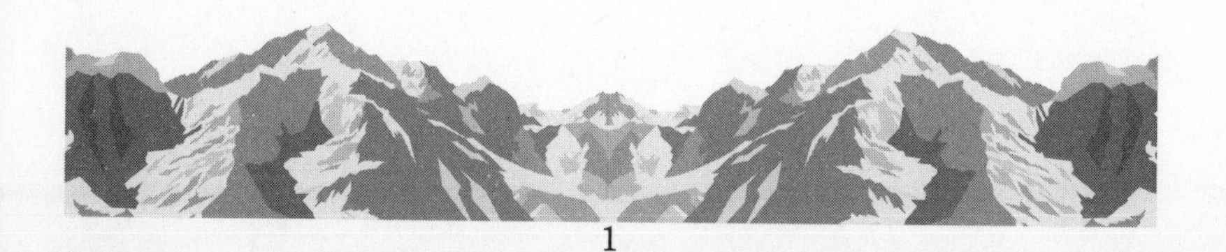

stood on end in several places as if a cow had licked its way across his head. "Down? DOWN?!" he muttered loud, then louder, as he rubbed his eyes and looked out the window of the Boeing 767.

"She means we're about to land," Mimi reassured him.

"Oh," said Grant, stretching. He pressed his nose flat against the cold window. "Hey, we're landing in the mountains!"

That comment made Mimi, Papa, Christina–and everyone nearby–stare out of the plane.

Papa shook his head. "I don't see what you mean, Grant."

Grant pointed downward. "See all the pointy, white peaks. That little mountain range."

Papa laughed; so did everyone else. Grant folded his arms across his chest and scowled. What had he said that was so funny, he wondered.

Mimi knew Grant was embarrassed. She patted him on the shoulder. "You're right, Grant. The Denver International Airport does look like a miniature mountain range, doesn't it? They made it in that style on purpose. The big tent peaks make you think of the famous Rocky Mountains."

Grant smiled, as if he knew that all along. Then, Christina pointed out the window and said, "Now THAT'S a mountain range!"

Everyone looked out at the sawtooth silhouette of a strip of endless white mountains covered in snow against a bright blue sky. It was beautiful.

Mimi laughed. "You're right! The Rocky Mountains are one of the most amazing and beautiful mountain ranges in the world. Even though I've written a lot about geology, it's still a mystery to me how something so majestic got created."

Christina frowned and cleared her throat. "Mimi," she said sternly, glaring at her grandmother from beneath arched eyebrows that seemed to say, *remember*?

"What?" asked Mimi, pretending to be aggravated, but Christina and Grant knew that she understood perfectly well what was meant. "WHAT?" Mimi repeated, teasing them.

Christina shook her head, her long brown hair slinging back and forth. "Don't even use that word!"

"What word?" Papa asked.

"What word?" Mimi asked.

Grant laughed. "The M-word!" he said. "Mystery!"

Christina scrunched back in her seat. Mimi was a

kid's mystery book writer. She and Grant were lucky to get to travel with their grandparents on research and writing trips, but somehow, Mimi almost always got involved in a real, live mystery. And, it always seemed like it was up to Christina and Grant to solve it.

Mimi just smiled, her blond hair sticking up like little mountain peaks. She continued to chew on her red marker pen while she pondered the yellow legal pad in her lap. "I have no idea what you're talking about," she said sweetly.

"Sure!" grumbled Christina.

"SURE!" repeated Grant.

"Hey, this is a winter vacation," Papa reminded them. "No mystery necessary."

"Welcome to Denver, the Mile High City!" the pilot said over the intercom system. *"We will be landing in a moment. It is sixteen degrees outside, so put on your winter duds, folks. Don't break a leg on the ski slopes. And come back to see us again, real soon, you hear?"*

2 Denver, the Mile High City!

"Can you hear me now? Can you hear me now?" Grant repeated over and over as he moved down the airport concourse, tugging his Scooby Doo suitcase behind him. A strip of underpants hung out one side where he had not gotten all his clothing tucked in good before he latched the suitcase.

"YES we can hear you!" Christina screamed at him. Indeed, the Denver airport was made up of an unusual and very pretty array of enormous white fabric peaks, sort of like a circus tent. Grant was busy walking ahead and checking the acoustics of the magnificent building by shouting back to the others to see if they could hear him, or his echo, in the unique building.

It was very cool in the airport and Christina

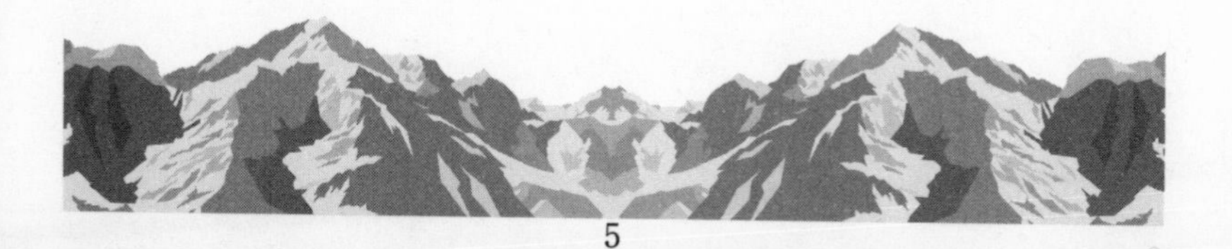

wondered what it might be like outside. She was not sure she had ever been in sixteen degree weather before. She tugged her pink Limited Two sweater more snugly around her neck. She was sure glad Mimi had bought them all some silky long underwear–"long johns," she called them. Her grandmother insisted that dressing in layers was the smart way to survive winter. Mimi did not like to be cold. Her other "big idea" was to drink lots of hot chocolate.

"Hey, let's stop here!" Mimi said. Sure enough it was a cute little kiosk that sold cocoa and cookies.

"I'll go get the rental car," Papa said. "You guys have a quick snack and meet me at the luggage carousel."

"We're getting our luggage at a merry-go-round?" Grant asked. As soon as he saw Mimi stop for food, he had come running back to join the others.

"No, silly," said Christina. "This carousel is that big metal conveyor belt that brings the luggage up from the airplane."

"Oh," said Grant, "that thing I like to ride on!"

"NO RIDING!" Mimi and Papa warned their grandson together. Grant just ducked his head and didn't say a word. Christina sighed. She knew that meant that Grant was making no promises not to misbehave. He just loved to explore first and think about danger later. As

soon as Christina thought of that word–danger–she wished she hadn't.

Papa sped off, loaded down with all Mimi's suitcases and computer and writing paraphernalia and the ski boots and skis loaded on a metal cart.

Mimi led the kids to a small silver table with snowflakes printed on it. They plunked down onto blue plastic chairs. Mimi told them to "stay put" while she got in line. Soon she reappeared with hot, steaming mugs of cocoa topped with big, square, homemade marshmallows. She also put down a small paper plate filled with sugar cookies. The sugar sprinkled on top of them glistened like the snow frosting the ground outside the window. Soon, their lips, cheeks, chin, and clothes glittered with the sprinkles as well.

"Delicious!" said Christina.

"GRMLISIUS!" Grant agreed, his mouth full. He sprayed Christina with a million tiny crumbs.

"GRANT!" she grumbled. Of course, crumbs spewed out of her mouth and plastered him. They both laughed. Grant laughed so hard that cocoa drizzled out of each corner of his mouth and dripped down his chin so that it looked like he had a funny, droopy mustache.

"If anybody asks me, I'm going to say I never saw

you two kids before," Mimi teased them. She tossed napkins at them both.

"Hey, Mimi," said Christina, "what's the plan?" Mimi always had a plan.

"Oh!" said Mimi, glad to be asked. She referred to her legal pad. "We're going to drive into Denver and spend the night at the famous and historic Brown Palace Hotel. We're going to LoDo and the Tattered Cover. Then we're going to Colorado Springs and see the Garden of the Gods and Pikes Peak. Next, we're headed for Durango. Then . . ."

When Mimi took a breath, Christina interrupted. "Mimi! When are we going to ski? To snowmobile? To sleep? To eat?"

"To go potty?" Grant interjected.

Mimi chuckled as she began to clean up the messy table. "Oh, we'll get it all in," she assured her grandchildren. "I have everything all planned out for our great Rocky Mountain vacation. Even going potty Grant–right over there." Mimi pointed to a door with the shape of a man on the front. "We'll meet you right there in a few minutes." Mimi pointed to a large Christmas tree where two big hallways came together.

It was the middle of December; school Christmas

break. Christina's and Grant's cousin, Zander, who was 11, and his sister, Dakota, who was 8, were going to meet them at the Brown Palace Hotel. They lived in Albuquerque, New Mexico, but were moving to Salt Lake City, Utah. After a few days of sightseeing and snowskiing, they all were supposed to return to Denver and fly home for the holidays.

Christina was excited, but a little nervous. She had never skied. She had never snowmobiled. She was a little afraid of heights. She'd heard a lot about avalanches of snow falling down the sides of mountains and burying people in the snow. But she liked new adventures, so, she told herself, this was going to be Fun, Fun, FUN. That is, IF Mimi's friends "mystery" and "danger" stayed back home in Peachtree City.

I'm being silly, Christina thought to herself. I'm the luckiest girl to be in Colorado for a wow winter vacation. Suddenly, she spotted Grant running around the Christmas tree, flapping his arms like a snow angel. He was singing "I'm Dreaming of a White Christmas" at the top of his lungs.

Christina ran to join him. She pulled her Lizzy McGuire suitcase behind her as fast as she could. "What are you so excited about?" she asked her brother.

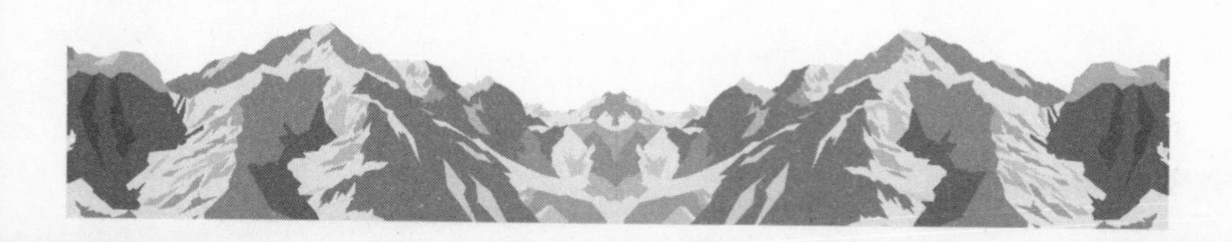

Grant continued to race around the tree singing. "Just look out the window!" he said.

Christina turned and looked out the big plate glass window to the airport runways. The mountain range in the distance had disappeared. Everything was white and frosty and foggy. And, it was SNOWING!

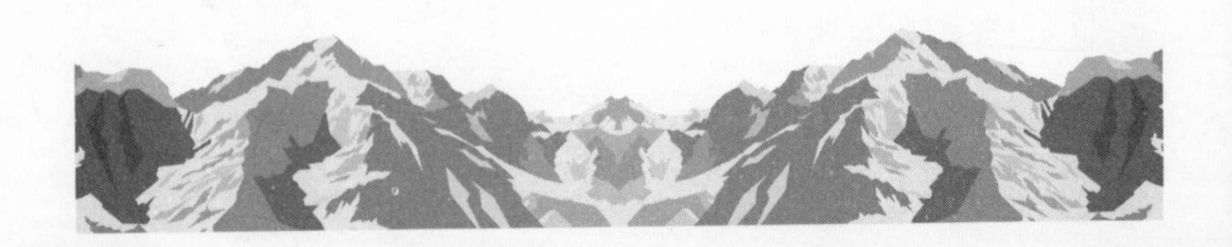

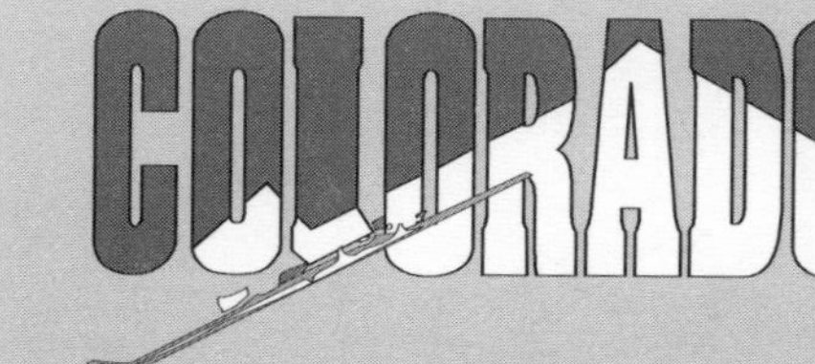

Wyoming
Nebraska
Rocky Mountain
National Park
Denver
Breckenridge
Utah
Kansas
Colorado Springs
Pike's Peak
MINE
Silverton
Mesa Verde
National Park
Durango
COLORADO
AZ
New Mexico
Oklahoma

3 The Brown Palace Hotel

When they met Papa, they saw he had rented the largest SUV they had ever seen. It was big and red and had a ski rack on top. He had everything loaded up, then quickly tossed the rest of the luggage Mimi, Christina, and Grant had into the back.

"Get in the car!" he said. "It's freezing out here!"

Fortunately the car was all warm. The heated seats felt wonderful on their backsides. A Christmas carol streamed out of the CD-player.

"This is an expensive rental car," Mimi noted.

"Aw, they gave me a special deal," said Papa.

"Why?" Mimi asked suspiciously.

"Because I'm so handsome!" Papa said and grinned. Christina laughed; Mimi just groaned.

"Too bad there's not a DVD," Grant commented.

Mimi groaned again. "This is a road trip," she said. "You're supposed to look out the window and see stuff you've never seen before."

"Well, I'm looking out the window," Grant argued, "and I don't see *anything!*"

"That is a problem," Papa agreed. It was now so foggy that even with the fog lights on, you could hardly see more than a few feet ahead.

It was like being in a fairytale ballet, Christina thought. Like the nutcracker in the scene where it snows. The *"Nutcracker"* was Christina's favorite ballet. She adored the story of Clara and the toy nutcracker she receives as a Christmas gift. Of course she knew Grant preferred the fighting mice and the funny Chinamen.

"Can we go see the *'Nutcracker'* again this year?" Christina asked Mimi from the back seat.

"Nutcracker! Butsmacker!" Papa grumbled. "I can't see a thing!"

Grant giggled, but Christina shushed him. They both knew when Papa was trying to drive they were supposed to "BE-HAVE!" Papa did not like distractions while he was driving, especially on the interstate highway. He always pulled off the road to talk on his cell phone. Of course, he almost never had to do that because Mimi

always had the cell phone glued to her ear. Usually she was talking to their Mom, or Uncle Michael, back at the office. When she was saying baby words like "Goo Goo, Gah, Gah, Coochie, Coochie, Coo," they knew she was talking to their cousin, Baby Avery, who was too little to come along with them yet on adventures.

But now, Mimi and Papa were both peering seriously out the front window. Papa said the fog was as thick as "pea soup." Mimi said it looked like "Old London Town." Neither comment made sense to Grant and Christina. They both loved watching the snow tumble down from the sky. How could you have too much snow, Christina wondered.

Soon, Papa pulled out on the interstate and the fog seemed to lift. Ahead, blue sky appeared and once more they could see the beautiful row of Rocky Mountains. In front of the jagged peaks stood Colorado's capital city, Denver.

"It's so flat here," said Christina. "How can Denver be a mile high?"

Now that Papa could see to drive, he was eager to talk. "It's measured from sea level," he explained. "We're just a few hundred feet above sea level back in Peachtree City. But out here, Denver is one mile above sea level."

"That's 5,280 feet!" said Grant, who was very good at math. He loved to play Monopoly®, count money, and he could even add and subtract negative numbers.

Christina rubbed her tummy. "I don't feel so good," she said.

"Too much cocoa?" Mimi asked.

"It's the altitude," Papa insisted. "It will take us all a little while to get used to the higher altitude. Rest, drink a lot of water, and don't run around like wild banshees," he recommended.

"Oh, great," said Christina. "A vacation and I get to be sick, in bed, and still."

"Running around like a wild banshee–whatever that is, Papa–is my favorite thing," Grant added.

"Oh, you'll be used to the altitude in no time," Mimi reassured them. "Think positive."

Soon, they were thinking positive as the snow continued to clear and the mountains seem to grow higher and higher before their very eyes. Denver looked like a fairytale city in the snow. Christina liked the look of the Cherry Creek Mall as they passed by. The parking lot was jammed with cars. She figured major Christmas shopping was going on inside. Both she and Mimi looked out the window wistfully.

"Don't even think about it," Papa said.

Mimi laughed. "I plan to shop till I drop, first chance I get!" she insisted.

Me, too!" Christina chimed in.

"Not me," said Grant. "I plan to ski till I, till I, till I pee!" When everyone laughed, Grant grumbled, "Well, it was the only word I could think of that rhymed."

Soon, they were in the city center. The layer of snow made everything seem quiet like a Sunday afternoon. Even the pedestrians, all bundled up from head to toe, seemed to move in slow motion. Suddenly Papa whisked the car through the slush into a parking place in front of a tall brick building with a large canopy awning out front.

A smartly dressed doorman opened Christina's door. "Welcome to the Brown Palace Hotel," he said. "You're just in time for tea!"

As the car was unloaded and everything piled onto a luggage cart, Mimi, Grant, and Christina scurried beneath the canopy into the lobby. Papa told the doorman, "Valet parking, please!" and hustled in behind them.

Perhaps that is why they did not notice the tiny, red beeping beeping beeping monitor that had been stuck beneath the bumper of the back of their rental car. Nor did they notice the two men in black trenchcoats with black

wool caps pulled down low over their eyebrows who had parked their beat-up black sedan at the curb, and followed them inside the hotel.

Inside the lobby of the Brown Palace Hotel, Christina and Grant both said the same thing: "Wow!"

The old hotel dated back to the Victorian era when men with whiskers and gold watches made millions of dollars from the gold and silver mines tucked into the nearby mountains. The rich and the famous had stayed at the "Brown" over the years.

"It really looks like a palace!" Christina whispered to Mimi, as Papa checked them into the hotel.

"It is palatial," Mimi agreed. She and Christina stared up at the enormous, glistening chandelier suspended from a nine-story high ceiling of colorful Tiffany glass. They rubbed their hands along the gleaming brass rail that ran around the fancy restaurant in the center of the lobby.

"Look!" said Christina, pointing discreetly to the white cloth-covered tables set with glass and silver, candles, and plates of fancy, little sandwiches in the shapes of triangles, squares, circles, and hearts. There

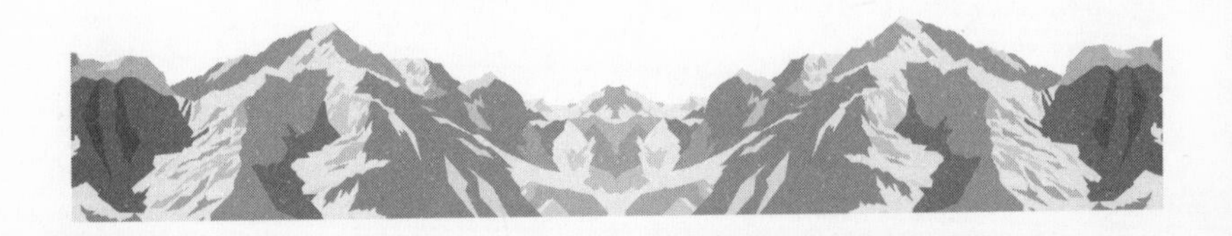

were also glass trays of tiny *petit fours*, or deserts, like cookies, brownies, and pink-frosted cakes. "It makes my mouth water!"

They were interrupted when Papa reappeared and handed Mimi a large brass key to their room.

"Why don't you ladies get dressed for tea," Papa suggested.

"Aren't you and Grant joining us?" Mimi asked.

"I think my man Grant and I are going to get the car and take a little tour by Coors Field, Mile High Stadium, and a few other guy-sites before it gets dark."

Grant giggled. "Yeah," he said, mainly to his sister. "I think I will pass on tea. Papa and I could go for a cold beer–root beer."

"Make sure it is," Mimi teased Papa, as he beckoned to the bellman to get their car. "And don't be long; it's supposed to start snowing even heavier later."

Grant and Papa just shrugged their shoulders like, "Big deal!"

Usually, Christina would argue about things being boy-stuff or girl-stuff. After all, she played soccer and basketball and liked sports too. And she knew for a fact that Grant and Papa loved little sandwiches and sweets. But on this special day, she was tickled pink as her sweater

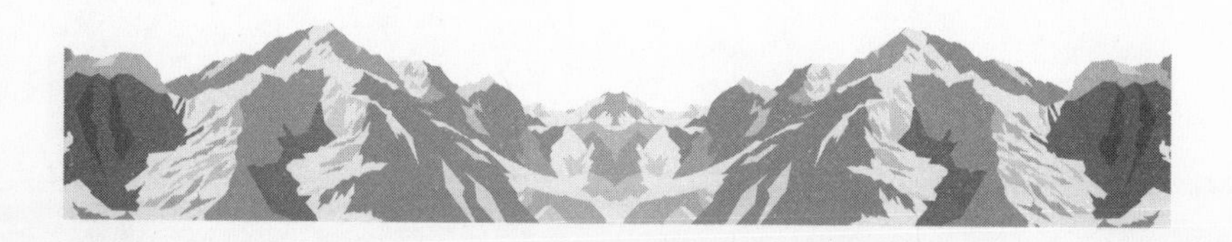

to have Mimi all to herself and to go to "high tea" just like all the Moms and grandmothers and girls she saw slurping their cocoa from tiny china cups right now. She could hardly wait to get dressed.

As she and Mimi headed for the elevator, Papa and Grant bundled back up and headed out into the snow. Just for a moment, Christina noticed that it appeared to be flashing pink beneath the back of the car. But she thought nothing of it, of course. As the big SUV sped off, she also noticed another car followed right behind it. Again, it did not arouse any suspicion in Christina's mind.

After all, this was a winter holiday, not a mystery.

Wasn't it?

4 What's a LoDo?

Upstairs, Christina went wild over their room. "Why it looks like the fancy hotel where Eloise lived!" she marveled. She meant the character Eloise from the books she had read about a trouble-making little girl who lived at the Plaza Hotel in New York City.

Christina was not happy until she had sat in every big, fat, overstuffed armchair, flopped down on the big canopy bed so tall that she had to climb three little steps to get into it, and oohed and aahed at the humongous clawfoot bathtub in the bathroom.

Mimi was filling the tub with steamy water. As she poured some pink gel beneath the faucet, bubbles began to boil up into a wintery, white froth that smelled like peppermint.

"Ooh, a bubblebath!" Christina said. She usually

took showers. “Me first, please?!” she begged.

“Fine by me,” said Mimi. “I want to set up my computer, anyway.”

It took Christina no time to take off her traveling clothes and slip down into the deep warm water. The bubbles came right up to her chin. She reached down and grabbed two handfuls of white foam and plopped them on her head like a hat.”

“Hey, Mimi, look at me!” she called.

Mimi poked her head in the bathroom and laughed. “Looks good on you,” she said. “Now don’t dawdle; tea doesn’t last all afternoon,” she reminded her granddaughter.

Since Christina certainly didn’t want to miss the big event, she quickly bathed, dried off, and put on one of the warm, thick, terrycloth robes hanging on the back of the bathroom door on a fancy hook. Even though the robe was too long for her, she managed to trudge through the room to sit in front of the fire in the marble fireplace for a few minutes before she got dressed.

“I’m liking winter better every minute,” she said, mostly to herself. “This is going to be a great vacation. I just know it is.” She glanced over at Mimi, but her grandmother was focused on her computer screen, already

writing a mystery book, set in Denver of course, at Christmas, of course, in the snow, of course, and starring Grant and Christina, OF COURSE!

Back downstairs, Christina and Mimi settled into their chairs at a corner table. Christina wondered why Mimi had insisted she bring her special dress and hat along on the trip. She felt so pretty. And Mimi looked beautiful in her purple silk dress and bright red hat.

Christina was glad she knew good etiquette. She put her cloth napkin in her lap and remembered to keep her elbows off the table.

"Would you like some hot chocolate, Miss?" a handsome young waiter asked. He held a large, flowered china teapot in the air.

"Yes, please," Christina managed to answer.

Her grandmother smiled at her approvingly. "And we'll be served now, please," Mimi said. The young man nodded and soon returned with their yummy-looking sandwiches and sweets.

"You're in luck," he whispered to them, as he set the plates down. "We have some very special entertainment this afternoon!"

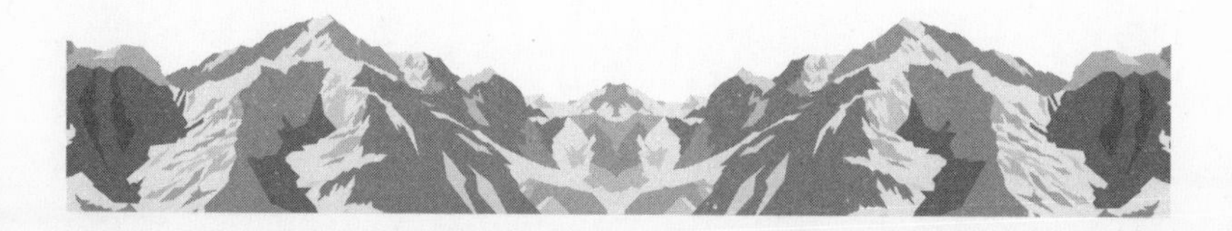

Suddenly, the lights in the room dimmed and a soft pink spotlight lit up an area near where Christina and Mimi sat. With no introduction, a woman dressed in a flouncy white dress and large straw hat appeared on the small stage. She held a fancy fan in one hand and waved it near her face as she began to speak. And this is what she said:

"Good afternoon. I have a story to tell you all. And once I have finished my tale of wonder and woe–the first person to guess who I am will receive a very special gift." The woman held up a small red box tied with a shiny red ribbon.

"Now," she continued. *"I was originally from Missouri. But in the early 1800s, I moved to Leadville, Colorado. This was the heyday of the discovery and mining of gold and silver–some of it still hiding–in the Rocky Mountains region. In 1886, I married a man named James Brown. He was in charge of the Little Johnny Mine. And . . ."* The woman jutted her chin in the air and sighed happily as she added . . . *"he was a millionaire!"*

The women in the room chuckled softly. Christina realized that the woman was actually an actress telling a story about someone from Denver's past. Everything she was saying was a clue. Christina hoped if she listened

Tea at the Brown Palace Hotel!

carefully, she might be able to figure out the answer and win the prize. She wondered what could be in the pretty red box. She was so captivated with the story that she almost forgot to eat and drink until Mimi poked her in the side and nodded down at her plate.

"I returned to Denver," the woman continued, sashaying back and forth across the stage as she told her tale. *"Mr. Brown built a beautiful mansion just up on the hill for me."* She waved her fan toward somewhere outdoors. *"He even put two large stone lions at the entrance of our wonderful home."*

"Now one day, I left Denver to go on an amazing adventure! I went to sail on the maiden voyage of the brand new ocean liner known as the Titanic. Now this was the most amazing ship of its day. It was the largest! And the swankiest! Everybody who was anybody was on board."

Mimi and Christina exchanged glances and smiles. You could tell that the woman really wanted everyone to know that she was truly a society somebody.

"Our trip got off to a fabulous start!" the woman continued. *"There were beautiful people and clothes, and dining and dancing. It was a dream come true! Until . . ."* When the actress said this word, the lights dimmed. She peered out into the darkened room and whispered:

"And then, as the ship was sailing through the North Atlantic Ocean, in waters filled with icebergs, there was a loud CRACK! Of course, none of the passengers heard this sound because we were fast asleep in our cabins. But soon, the cry went round the ship that we had struck an iceberg and the ship was sinking!

"As you might imagine, there was great panic. The Titanic was said to be unsinkable, yet here it was sinking. People scrambled into lifeboats. It was women and children first. The men stayed on board.

"Soon, all the lifeboats were filled. But there were not enough lifeboats, so many people remained on board and died when the ship finally sank. Those of us on lifeboats were freezing. It was nighttime and it was bitterly cold. No one was coming to rescue us. We drifted apart. When people on my boat began to wail and cry, I told them to hush up. I told them we would survive if we were brave and stuck together. I shared my clothes with some of the other women and children. I screamed at the helmsman to row faster or move over and I would row!"

This made the women in the audience laugh a little, but Christina felt like she could cry, the story was so horrible. A small voice in the darkness asked, "What happened?" The actress went on in her dramatic fashion,

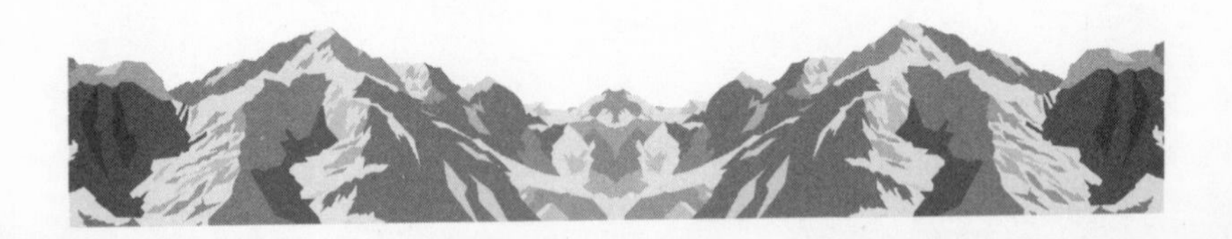

as if she had not heard the question.

"It was morning before we were rescued. The death toll was enormous. But they finally got us–we were like wet, frozen rats!–onto another ship. And I came home–back to Denver. IT WAS A MIRACLE!"

"NOW!" she said, snapping her fan closed, and waving the lights to come up. *"Tell me who I am, someone. I am famous. I am the famous . . . the remarkable . . ."*

"The Unsinkable Molly Brown!" Mimi shouted.

Everyone applauded. Mimi nodded her red hat modestly at the crowd. Christina clapped loudest of all.

The actress stepped forward. "Of course I am!" she said proudly. She presented Mimi with the red box. Then she took a bow, the audience applauded loudly, and the woman disappeared behind the stage curtain. The lights came back up.

"Mimi!" Christina said. "How did you know that?"

"Why that's one of the most famous stories in history," Mimi said. "I'm sure you will study it in school one day." With a flourish, Mimi handed the red box to Christina. "Merry Christmas!"

"Oh," said Christina, taking the box. "I can't take that. You won the prize fair and square. I didn't have a clue."

Mimi laughed. "Oh, Christina, you always have

clues! Open the box and enjoy it."

Christina couldn't resist. She slipped the red ribbon off and tugged the red silk lid off the box. It was filled with gold tissue paper. Something heavy was wrapped inside. Gently, Christina pulled the paper away. There was a stone heart just about the size of her hand. Inscribed on it in beautiful writing which said: "May life always be a wonderful mystery to you!"

Christina didn't know whether to laugh or cry. She just shook her head slowly and looked up at Mimi. "Thank you," she said. Then under her breath, she added, "I think."

The next day was the busiest ever. Everyone was up early. There was a lot of snow, but the sun was shining brightly. Zander and Dakota arrived bright and early. They had traveled alone on an early flight to the Denver airport and taken a shuttle into town. Christina thought they were very brave to travel alone. Grant thought they had really grown a lot since he had seen them last.

"Are you older?" Grant asked, as they stood in the lobby of the hotel.

"Of course!" Dakota said, with a laugh. "It's been a

whole year since we've seen you guys. I'm in third grade now and Zander is in fifth. You look a lot bigger yourself."

Grant stood up as tall as he could. "Yeah," he said. "I'm seven now. And Christina's nine. I guess we'll all be teenagers before you know it."

"Not so soon, young man," said Mimi.

"Yes, yes, soon!" said Papa, who had not even heard their conversation. "This is our only day in Denver. We've got to get out of here and get busy."

Everyone dashed around putting on jackets and hats and mittens. Their boots squished on the marble floor. Papa led the way through the revolving glass door and they plunged from the warmth of the lobby to the frigid weather outdoors.

"Which way?" asked Mimi.

"This way to LoDo," said Papa, leading the way.

"What's a LoDo?" asked Christina.

"It's an abbreviation for Lower Downtown," Papa called back to them.

"It's where the Tuba Concert and the Tattered Cover are," Mimi explained, only none of that made any sense to the kids. They just followed along, trying to stay caught up with Papa's long-legged stride, and trying to jump over icy puddles instead of splatting into them.

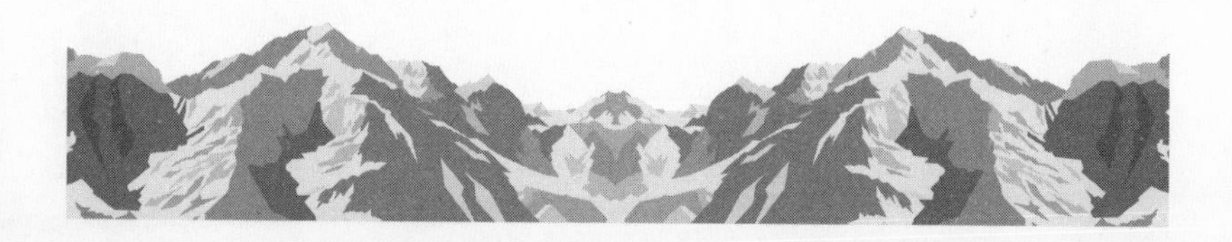

All except Grant that is, who couldn't resist a puddle if he tried.

"You should have been a duck," Zander told Grant.

Grant just looked at his cousin like he was blind. "I am a duck, silly!" he said, and splatted twice in the nearest puddle. He splashed down so hard that icy mud splattered on the pants leg of two men following close behind them.

"Darn," the tall man said.

"Don't say bad words," Grant said merrily to no one in particular.

But the man knew who Grant meant. "Just shut up kid," the man groused. But Grant didn't hear him because he had sped ahead and caught up with Papa to lead the way to LoDo.

5 Too Many Tubas!

They traipsed down the Sixteenth Street Mall to Larimer Square. Soon they were in the middle of the popular "LoDo" area. The streets were filled with Christmas shoppers, Santas, lots of families, especially children, and a lot of musicians carrying tubas.

Everything was decorated gaily for the holidays. There was a wonderful smell of hot pretzels baking on an outdoor oven. Many people had their mittened or gloved hands wrapped around steaming cups of hot chocolate or apple cider.

In spite of the cold, shop doors were open as people dashed from shop to shop. Mimi peered into one window which had a display of beautiful silver and turquoise Native American Indian jewelry. Papa was busy admiring a saddle and a pair of cowboy boots in another shop window.

Suddenly Grant began to squeal, "Can we? Can we? Can we, please?"

Everyone turned to see that he had spotted an outdoor ice rink located between two brick buildings. Even though it was crowded, it looked like it could hold a few more skaters.

Christina, Zander, and Dakota joined in the pleading. But it was not necessary.

"We've got about an hour before the tuba concert," said Papa. "So, let the Games begin!" He handed them each a five dollar bill, the cost of admission to the rink, including a pair of skates.

By the time the kids got their skates on, the crowd had thinned out a little bit as people gathered down the street for the upcoming concert. It was just as well, Christina thought. Here were four kids who had never ice skated before, so they needed plenty of room to slide around, hold on, and FALL!

Zander was the best. He zipped across the ice like he knew what he was doing. Christina tried her best, but she preferred to hover near the side rail where she could grab hold quickly if she felt herself falling. Dakota took baby steps, then went into a skid and fell on her backside. She looked like she didn't know whether to laugh or cry.

In the meantime, Grant was his usual fearless self. He skated in a zigzag pattern back and forth across the ice. When he fell, he just laughed and popped right back up like a jack-in-the-box. When he skidded into another unsuspecting skater, he muttered "S'cuse me," and skated on. Pretty soon he was covered in streaks of ice and zooming faster and faster across the ice, either on his feet, belly, or bottom–it really didn't seem to matter to him.

Christina enjoyed watching her brother. She made him laugh. He was so silly. It was like he was enjoying his own private Ice Capades. She wished she weren't so self-conscious, but she'd rather stay on her feet and at least look like she was skating, if at all possible.

While she held onto the rail, laughing at her brother, a man outside on the sidewalk tapped her on the shoulder. Christina turned to see a short man in a black trenchcoat with a black hat (what Mimi would call a watchcap) pulled almost down over his eyes. Behind him stood a tall man who was dressed exactly the same way.

"Here, missy," the man in front said in a growly voice. "Take this, wouldya?" He thrust a wadded piece of paper into Christina's mitten, then both men turned on their heels and raced across the street and disappeared into the crowd.

"What's that all about?" Zander asked suspiciously. "You know those two guys?"

"No, I do not," said Christina. "But they seem to think they know us, or me at least. Or, it's some kind of case of mistaken identity."

She unfolded the wadded up note. It was really an old ski ticket, the kind they fasten to your jacket after you pay your money at the ski slope. Every time you went up the lift, they scanned your ticket with a little handheld scanner so they would know how many visitors they had that day, and, to be sure they had paid.

"Those dudes don't look like skiers," Zander noted.

"They look like a couple of thugs to me," Christina said. She handed the ski ticket to Zander to read.

"We're gonna be watching you guys!" he read aloud. "Now why would they be watching us?"

Christina shook her head, making her pink cap bounce on her head. "I think they must be crazy," she said. "I think I saw them at the hotel, but I think they must just be a couple of clowns or have the wrong people."

"This is not one of your Grandmother Mimi's famous mysteries, is it?" Zander asked.

Christina bent down to take off her skates. "No," she said. "I'm certain it's not. Like I said, a case of

mistaken identity, or something. Let's don't worry about it. And let's don't say anything or it will only make Mimi and Papa worry."

"And watch us even closer," said Zander.

Christina giggled. "Yeah, and we never want that!"

Suddenly, they were surprised by Papa who leaned over the ice skating rink rail and said, "Time's up, you guys. Get your shoes back on. The concert is about to start. You won't want to miss this!"

Quickly, the kids put on their boots and returned their skates. They held onto one another as they wove their way through the crowd until they finally found Mimi and Papa on the corner. Papa had saved them a good place right in front of the tuba band, so they could see–and hear–everything.

Christina had never seen so many tubas in her life. She thought that would be the last instrument she would ever want to play in a band. It was big and heavy, and, she guessed, difficult to learn to play. She much preferred her piano lessons.

The big brass tubas glistened in the sun. There were little tubas, and big tubas, and gigantic tubas. The band members wore matching red and white sweaters and hats that said "TUBA" on them. They seemed jolly and

excited to be standing in the cold preparing to play for such a big and happy Christmas crowd.

"Hey, won't their lips stick to that thing?" Grant asked, indicating the mouthpiece. Without waiting for an answer, he added, "Hey, look! I don't need a tuba to play." He held his belly and began to belt out a sound that was sort of tuba-sounding. Only it sounded really bad.

Dakota giggled. "Grant, you are so silly!" she said, but it was in admiration.

"Hush up, you guys," Papa said. "They're about to begin."

And, sure enough, with a whisk of the band leader's baton, almost 500 tuba players began to play Jingle Bells. Christina thought it was the wildest thing she had ever heard. It was really loud, and really deep, and surprisingly in tune. She figured you could hear the concert all the way over to the edge of the mountains.

Everyone in the crowd began to laugh and applaud. It was clear that the tuba concert was a real holiday favorite that local people showed up to hear again and again each Christmas season.

After what seemed like a hundred songs, the tuba players took a bow and the crowd began to drift away down side streets to their cars or to shops or restaurants.

"How did you like that?" Mimi asked the kids.

"Pretty cool," said Zander.

"It was fun," Dakota agreed.

"I liked the big deep-sounding tubas the best," Christina added.

"Grant?" Papa asked, when his grandson had made no comment. "What did you think?"

Grant put his hand under his chin and tilted his head thoughtfully. "I think there were too many tubas," he said. "Waaaaaaay too many tubas!"

They all laughed. "I'm getting cold," Christina complained.

"Yes," Mimi agreed. "I think the temperature must be dropping. We were in the sun and now the shade is here between the buildings. I'm freezing, too."

"Well, have no fear," said Papa. "See right down that little alley? I parked our SUV over there earlier this morning. By the time you get there, I'll have it warm. We'll go have some lunch." Papa ran across the street, dodging the rest of the tuba players and concertgoers.

In spite of being cold, the rest of them took their time crossing the street, stopping to look in shop windows. Christina remembered that she had not finished her Christmas shopping. She hoped there would be time to

shop later. But right now, they saw Papa waving them over and so they hurried to the car.

As they all climbed in, once more, no one noticed the red flasher beacon that was just beneath the car, held there by a magnet. Nor did they notice the two men in the beat-up black sedan following them yet again.

But why?

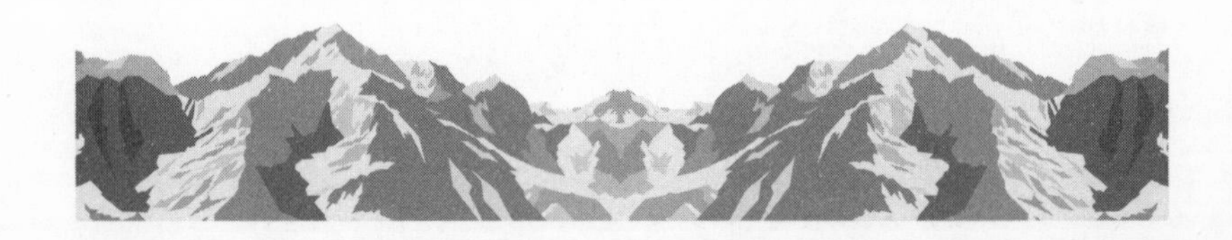

Waaaaaaayy too many tubas!

6 Torn Up at the Tattered Cover

The big SUV bounced along the brick-paved streets. LoDo had once been a dumpy, run-down part of town. But in the last few years, it had gotten really fixed up with neat loft apartments and condos. There were shops, and restaurants, and little parks, and gaslights on every corner.

Papa parked in front of a neat-looking restaurant and they went inside. The chairs were really stools with horse saddles on top of them.

"Yipeeyi, kai, yo!" Grant hollered as he climbed into his seat.

"Hey, this is cool," said Zander, sticking his foot into a stirrup and pulling himself up.

Papa lifted Dakota up and put her on a seat.

Mimi sat "side-saddle."

Papa looked at Christina with his thick, black eyebrows raised, as if to ask, "You want a lift up or not?"

But Christina had already put her foot in a stirrup and tried to get up. For some reason, she wasn't having any luck.

"You gotta get up on the left side," Zander told her.

"You mean left is right?" Christina asked.

"Yep," said Papa, who wore cowboy boots and a cowboy hat and was sitting tall in his saddle, ready to order. "Left is right and right is wrong."

"Now I really am confused," Christina said with a laugh, but she switched sides and got up easily.

They ordered bison burgers, which Papa told them were made from buffalo meat. And a mountain of French fries and onion rings. And large chocolate shakes all around.

"Eat up," Mimi said. "We have to check out of the hotel soon, and I have one more stop I want us to make before we leave town."

"What's that?" asked Christina, hoping it was a mall.

"A bookstore," Mimi said.

"But not just any old bookstore, right Mimi?" Christina asked. Mimi was very particular about her bookstores.

"Actually, Christina, it really is an old bookstore," Mimi said. "You could say it's tattered."

That didn't sound like much fun to the kids. Christina figured it was a used bookstore. She had heard Papa say there were a lot of neat used bookstores around where you could find first editions and collector's items and one-of-a-kind books. She was afraid that if they went in a store like that, they would never leave Denver. Papa did love his books. Mimi loved to research. Christina loved to read, but she did like to leave a bookstore or library in two hours or less, but you never knew if you went with her grandparents. They told her that one time they had spent the night in a bookstore, but she didn't know whether to believe them or not.

While Papa paid and Mimi went to the cowgirls' restroom, the kids began to twist and turn on their horses. Grant finally succeeded in riding his horse backwards which made Dakota laugh.

Then Christina noticed that Grant had a funny look on his face. He was staring out the restaurant window. And staring inside, their faces pressed to the glass, were those doggone men again. They held up a dirty piece of paper and motioned for Christina to come closer.

Out of curiosity, she did. The note said,

"Remember, we are watching you constantly."

Bravely, Christina looked up at the two weird men. She mouthed the word, "Why?" at them. But before they could answer, they must have spied Mimi and Papa coming back and they ran off.

"Gonna tell your grandparents now?" Zander asked.

"No!" Christina said stubbornly.

Fortunately, they were all distracted by Grant who was singing at the top of his lungs, "I'm an old cowhand, from the tuba band, and I like to blow up a lotta snow."

Mimi just ignored him and motioned for the other kids to climb down and head out the door. As Papa passed by, he picked Grant up off his horse, and the singing cowboy sang all the way to the car.

Mimi was, and wasn't, kidding about the bookstore, which was just around the corner. It was called the Tattered Cover. It did look old, but the books inside were new. If they had gone to lunch to get warm, it seemed like everyone else had wandered into the Tattered Cover.

Christina thought it was unlike any other bookstore she had ever been in. It was a conglomeration of large rooms, sort of spilling all over the place, like a large

mansion. The floors were wooden with some well-worn oriental carpets spread out in different places. A wide staircase with creaky stairs led up to the upper floors. There was also an elevator. And a coffee bar. And books, books, books, everywhere. And, there were lots of big armchairs, where people sat reading, just like they were in their own home.

"We'll meet right here in thirty minutes," Mimi told them. She pointed to a table at the edge of the coffee bar. "I'll buy anyone any book that does not cost more than ten dollars."

That was all the kids needed to hear. Mimi and Papa disappeared in the the Adult Non-Fiction section. Christina asked a clerk, "Where's the children's section?"

They followed the clerk's directions and soon found themselves in booklover's heaven, as far as Christina was concerned. She loved all bookstores, but this one seemed to have a lot to offer. All her old favorites were here, and then lots of new stuff she had never seen. Pretty soon, each of the kids was lost in the stacks looking for something to buy to read on the road to Colorado Springs.

When they finally gathered again at the front of the kid's section, they plopped down on a rug and Christina checked each book to see if the price was right, according

to what Mimi had said they could each purchase.

"Let's see," Christina said:

"Dakota: *It Happened in the Rocky Mountains*
Zander: *Rocky Mountain Nature Almanac*
Grant: *Tales, Trails, and Tommyknockers*
Christina: *Rocky Mountain Folklore*

I think Mimi will go for all those. Let's head back downstairs."

As the four kids scampered down the wooden staircase, they did not pay much attention to the two men in the black trenchcoats and watchcaps who charged up the steps. They appeared to be in a great hurry, heads down, arms swinging.

"Hurry up!" one man said to the other. "We gotta get some maps. I overheard our suspect saying they were heading out for Colorado Springs in just a few minutes."

The man trailing him groused, "I never bargained for all this."

"Bargain, shmargain, you're stuck with it now," the first man said. "Just gotta keep those nasty, nosy, know-it-all kids outta the way."

"How you gonna do that?" the second man asked.

The first man snickered evilly as he yanked a map from the rack, tearing it. "You just watch!"

7 It's Snowing!

Christina guessed it was obvious that they were from the South since they got excited every time a few flakes of snow floated down from the sky. But they couldn't help it–it almost never snowed back home, and when it did, it had sticks and stuff poking up out of the snow so it wasn't really beautiful like the snow up here. Of course she knew snow could be treacherous too. It sure made driving hazardous. Blizzard conditions limited visibility to virtually zero. And then there were those pesky avalanches.

They had checked out at the Tattered Cover and checked out of the Brown Palace Hotel, and now, in the late afternoon snow, they were heading down Interstate 25 toward Colorado Springs. All Christina really knew about Colorado Springs was that Mimi and Papa had lived there one time, Pikes Peak was nearby, the U.S. Air Force

Academy was there, and, it was where some lucky kids got to train in ice skating and other winter Olympic sports.

The four kids were hunkered down in the back of the SUV snuggled between the heated seats and the woolly black and blue plaid blanket Mimi had brought along for them. Between the soft filtered light overhead and the white glare of the snowy outdoors, they were able to read their books. Occasionally one of them shared something of interest:

"My book says the long, unbroken stretch of mountains we see off to our right is called the Front Range," Dakota said. "Some of the mountain peaks are more than 14,000 feet high. They call those the Fourteeners and people like to climb them. I can't imagine what that's like!"

"You'll find out soon," Mimi said from the front seat. She had her laptop open and was typing away. "We're not going to climb Pikes Peak, but we're going to drive up it tomorrow!"

The kids were quiet, thinking about that adventure, when Zander piped up. "My book talks about all the flora and fauna in the Rocky Mountains. "You know," he added, when Grant gave him a puzzled look, "the birds, and the bees, and the flowers, and the trees. There are antelope,

bats, bears, bighorn sheep, bison, coyote, dinosaurs, eagles, moose, prairie dogs, rattlesnakes, vultures, wolves, and tarantulas."

"Whoa!" said Grant, "there aren't any dinosaurs anymore."

"Not above ground," said Papa from the front seat. "But beneath the earth in Arizona, Colorado, Utah–beneath all the Rocky Mountains–there are loads of dinosaur fossils."

"And what about those tarantulas? They're just fossils too, right?" Christina asked hopefully.

Zander was pleased to inform her: "Nope! Those suckers are alive and kickin' and just waitin' for some poor, unsuspectin' little flatlander girl to accidentally grab one up in the palm of her hand!"

"YIIIIIIIIII!" the girls squealed, kicking the blanket until it fell to the floor.

"Settle down back there," Papa warned. "It's hard enough to drive in a blizzard without a bunch of tommyknockers in the back seat going wild."

"It's snowing so hard, I can't even see to backseat drive," Mimi said.

"Well, that's one advantage of a blizzard," Papa said.

The kids pulled the blanket back up over their legs.

"What's a tommyknocker?" Christina asked.

Grant waved his hand in the air like he was in class, wanting to answer a question. "I know! I know!" he said. "I just read it in my book. Listen: *Miners in the Rockies believed in tommyknockers. These were tiny men who were said to be the spirits of dead miners. Miners didn't really see the tommyknockers, but they heard their tap-tap-tapping on the walls of the mine. When they followed the sound of this tapping, they often found a rich vein of ore.*"

"Is that true?" Christina asked Mimi.

"Well, it's a real myth," Mimi said. "Old mining folklore. Is it true? What do you kids think?"

"Yeeeeeessssssssss!" hollered the boys.

"Noooooooooooooooo!" the girls squealed.

"You know what is true," said Papa. "They used to lower a cage with a canary in it down into the mines. When they pulled the cage back up, if the canary was still alive, the miners knew it was safe to go to work down in the mines. If the poor bird was dead, they knew that the air was too bad to safely go into."

"What did they mine here?" Zander asked.

"Oh, I read that in my book," Christina answered. "Gold and silver and zinc and other stuff like something

called molybdenum. The mines all had neat names like Cripple Creek, Gold Hill, and Silver Plume. Not only that, even though the Gold Rush out here was really back in the mid-1800s, they still mine for gold and silver and other things in the Rockies today."

"Hey, Papa," said Mimi sweetly. "Will you buy me a gold mine for a souvenir while we're out here?"

Papa likes to really ham things up. "Sure, honey pot!" he said in a cowpoke voice. "I'll buy you a bunch of mines and we'll leave these little tommyknockers we've got in the back seat out here to work 'em. Maybe they can pay their own way through college."

The kids giggled. Then, suddenly, they gasped. Their car jolted ahead–bumped from behind by another car. Fortunately, Papa was driving slow and held on tightly to the steering wheel and they just kept going.

"That guy behind us should slow down!" Papa said angrily. "You can't see a thing out there. I just hope we get to Colorado Springs before they close the road."

The kids sprung up on their knees and twisted around to look out the frosty back window. As the windshield wiper swiped the hurling snow away they could briefly see the vehicle behind them. It was a black sedan. In the front seat were two men, both in trenchcoats, and

both with black hats pulled down over their foreheads and eyebrows.

"Gonna tell now?" Zander whispered to Christina.

Christina looked pale. She turned around and sat back down. "Papa," she said. "We're being followed."

Papa just laughed. "I know," he said. "And way too closely."

"No," said Christina, "I mean we're really being followed."

Papa still didn't understand or believe her. "I can take care of that!" he said. Out the window, the "COLORADO SPRINGS" exit sign appeared. Papa put on his turn signal and swerved toward the exit ramp.

As they headed into the town, Christina looked back to see if the black car was still behind them, but it was snowing harder. Big. Fat. Endless flakes. As darkness came on, it gave Christina an eerie feeling. Like they were lost. Or invisible. Or something was about to happen. *Something bad.*

8 Colorado Springs

They didn't stay in a hotel this night. When they got to the edge of the city, Papa pulled into the parking lot of a motel with a big, neon cactus for a sign. The motel was made of cocoa-colored adobe and had wooden vigas sticking out from the roof. The snow on the terra cotta tile roof made the building look like a giant frosted gingerbread cookie.

While Papa checked in, the kids dashed from the car, trying to take everything in one trip–and they were still covered in snow! Inside room 13 (Christina's least favorite room number!), they stamped the snow from their feet and piled their luggage in the corner.

"Mimi, this place is so cool!" Christina said.

"Oh, I'll put a log on the fire," Mimi promised.

Christina looked over at the cute kiva fireplace built

into the wall in a soft, rounded shape. "I don't mean that kind of cool," she said. "I meant like really neat."

"Yes," said Mimi. "I like this Old West Santa Fe style myself. It's comfy and cozy with the warm earth tones of the colors–gold and bronze and turquoise."

"Why did they make buildings of adobe in the olden days?" Dakota asked.

"There weren't any trees," Zander told his sister. "All the trees on the plains were cut down to make farmland. But you could mix mud and water and straw and make adobe."

Mimi and Papa had gone into the adjoining room to unpack. In this room, the girls picked one of the big beds and the boys took the other. Soon, everyone had their jackets and boots back on and scampered through the snow to the restaurant. Christina looked around for the black sedan, but did not see it.

At dinner, everyone ate heaping bowls of spicy chili, hot buttered rolls, and for desert, apple pie with vanilla ice cream on top.

"Sun'll be out tomorrow, amigos," the waiter told them. Christina had her doubts. Out the windows, the snow beat down upon the building as if insisting it wanted to come inside too and get warm.

Back in the room, the kids were too tired and full to read. They got into bed and turned out the lights. The kiva fire's red/black embers winked at them like dark, evil eyes. Christina slept, dreaming of men in black covered in snow, frozen in place like when you play the game Freeze Tag.

Too cold to camp outside!

9 Garden of the Gods

The next morning, the kids were amazed to see that the waiter had predicted correctly: the sun was shining so brightly against the white snow and the blue sky that they all had to put on sunglasses, so they wouldn't go "snow blind," Mimi said.

After big bowls of oatmeal with raisins and brown sugar and butter and cold glasses of orange juice, they all hopped into the SUV and went to explore Colorado Springs. As always, the Front Range of the Rocky Mountains made a jagged white silhouette on the horizon.

Soon Papa turned the car into an amazing place.

"Is this the Garden of the Gods?" Grant asked.

Papa opened the sunroof of the car and the kids jumped up to stare in wonder at the blood red rock formations that jutted up from the earth in strange

shapes and forms.

"What a great place to rock climb," said Zander.

"The Rocky Mountains are all about geology," said Mimi. "You'll be amazed at all the different types of rocks and geologic features you'll see. Mother Nature has had a good time over time! Wind, weather, water, and volcanic activity have rearranged the landscape a lot in the last million or billion years."

"I'll say!" Grant agreed. "Look at those two rocks. They look like kissing camels."

"And that one looks like a weeping Indian," said Christina.

"Can we get out and walk?" asked Dakota.

"Sure!" said Papa. He parked in a small parking area. He and Mimi pulled out their ever-present thermos of coffee. The kids hopped out of the car and took off toward the snow-covered rocks.

While the kids were exploring, a black car pulled in the other end of the parking area. The two men inside gave the SUV a hard look. Beneath the back-end of the car, the flasher steadily beeped its pink *beep*.

"We got a bead on them," the driver said. "Let's go get some breakfast. Then we'll catch up with them. No way they can get away from us now." The second man, still

half asleep, just nodded.

Christina, Grant, Zander, and Dakota had a great time hiking around the endless array of funny red slabs, mushrooms, "hoodoos," and other formations of rocks. It was too slippery with the snow to get up very high.

"This is a great place to play cowboys and Indians," Grant said.

"I'll bet there really were cowboys and Indians here at one time," Zander said thoughtfully. "Wonder where they are today?"

"Well, you'll see cowboys out on the ranches," Christina speculated. "And Papa said the Native Americans don't just live on reservations anymore. He said you're just as likely to meet one in the courthouse, the casino, or as a CEO running a business."

Christina and Grant were part Cherokee, and proud of their Indian heritage. Just as they were starting to brag about it, Dakota interrupted them.

"There they are!" she said. And, sure enough, the mysterious black sedan had appeared on the road that circled the Garden of the Gods.

"Let's get back in the car," Christina said. "It's

getting cold anyway. And don't say anything about those creepy guys. I'm going to figure this out before I try to explain to Mimi and Papa again that we're being followed."

Just as they reached the SUV, Papa flashed the car lights. They were ready to go. The kids clambered back in the back seat, snippets of snow and red rock dust clinging to their shoes and pants.

"Pikes Peak or bust!" Papa hollered.

"Why did you say that?" Christina asked.

"That's what everyone said who was headed to the gold and silver fields," Mimi explained. "They meant that they were determined to get here or die."

"And some of them did die?" Grant asked.

"It was a long, hard journey," Papa said, as he turned on the Pikes Peak Highway. "Remember, America was still pretty new back in the early 1800s. A lot of what the United States had bought in the Louisiana Purchase had never been explored."

It was hard to miss Pikes Peak. It was a "Fourteener" for sure. Jutting practically straight up out of the flat plain, the mountain towered over everything around it.

At first the drive up the curvy road just seemed like a Sunday drive through a forest. But soon, the road grew steeper and the hairpin turns twisted tighter and tighter.

"Whoa!" said Grant. "I hope we don't fall off over the side."

They all peered down the steep cliff wall of the mountain to what now appeared a tiny toy town far below.

But the road grew steeper yet. The car's engine sputtered. Christina grumbled that she couldn't breathe very good. Grant said his head hurt. Papa said to just hang on, they'd be to the top soon. Mimi looked nervous.

Soon, the car rounded a final turn and ran up over the gravel parking area at the top of the mountain. When they got outside, they were shocked to feel how much colder it was at this altitude and how hard the wind was blowing.

"Look fast!" Mimi urged. She snapped a quick digital photo of the group.

The view was magnificent. It was just like being on top of the world. Christina thought she had never seen such a beautiful sight. Maybe she could see all the way back to Georgia and over to California? Maybe she would freeze to death? Or throw up? She was the first to dash back into the car, but the others followed quickly.

On the way back down, everyone was pretty quiet. Christina thought about how amazing America was and how lucky she and Grant were to get to go with Mimi and Papa on adventures, mysteries or no mysteries.

About halfway down, Papa pulled over at a water fountain.

"Hey, read this historic marker!" Christina said when they got out.

The other kids ran over. Zander read aloud:

When Katherine Lee Bates passed this way in 1893, she was so impressed with the beauty of the Rocky Mountains and its red, sandstone foothills that she wrote the poem that was made into the song, America the Beautiful.

In spite of being out of breath, the kids astounded Mimi and Papa by singing as loud as they could:

"Oh, beautiful for spacious skies,
For amber waves of grain.
For purple mountain majesties
Above the fruited plain–
America, America, God shed his grace on thee,
And crown thy good with brotherhood
From sea to shining sea!"

Tourists who had gathered around applauded. The

kids did a quick bow or curtsey and jumped back in the car. As they got back on the road, Christina noticed the black sedan headed toward them. That car did not have four-wheel-drive, and so it was sort of slip-sliding up the mountain. The men inside looked panicky and frowned when they saw Christina looking at them out the window.

Christina couldn't help herself. She knew that since they'd passed up the mid-point stop, they'd have to go all the way to the top of the mountain to turn around. So, she did something silly, or maybe even stupid–only time would tell–she stuck her tongue out at them!

10 Dude, It's Durango!

The next stop on Mimi's and Papa's "Rocky Mountain Tour" was the old western town of Durango. As they drove slowly down the quaint Main Street, Christina could see a mix of what looked like tourist cowboys and real Native Americans.

They heard honky-tonk piano music wailing out of one saloon, and spotted horses parked in front of a Tack, Feed, and Seed store nearby. Suddenly, in the near distance, they saw an enormous plume of blue/gray steam spew up into the sky like a giant smoke signal.

"Is that it?" Grant screeched in excitement. "Is that the train?"

No one had to answer, since Papa pulled into the depot train station parking area. They watched in awe as the restored Durango and Silverton Narrow Gauge Railroad

huffed and puffed to a stop.

"Boy, we got here just in time," said Zander.

They sat there staring into the face of a cute, little train . . . led by one mean-looking engine that seemed to glow with fire. Its headlamp stared out at them, almost as if it was challenging them, "Ride me!"

But Papa already had tickets. "I wanted you kids to see how people got around in the early days out here," he said. "The local railroads from one mining town to another were real lifelines–that is, until they were run off by the development of the bigger railroads that only connected the big cities."

"Then what did you do?" asked Grant, collecting his things.

"Then you might ride your horse, or a mule or burro, or later, maybe take a carriage. The Rocky Mountains didn't make transportation a pleasure!"

"I think Papa just wants to hear me squeal when we go over the high mountain bridges or around the sharp curves on the steep cliffs," Mimi admitted.

"We're going to do those things?" Dakota asked hesitantly.

"It'll be fun!" Zander said.

"Oh, it will be an adventure, all right," Christina

agreed, giving the rest of the kids a big nod toward the train. They looked to see the two trenchcoat guys climbing into one of the cars..

Mimi and Papa were preoccupied with their thermos and cameras and did not notice the men.

"ALL ABOARD!!!!!!!!!!!" shouted the conductor. Afraid of literally "missing the train," they dashed toward the depot and boarded the train.

As it turned out, Mimi's and Papa's seats were at the front of the train. The kids' tickets were at the back. Mimi was not at all happy about this, but the conductor assured her that he would "look after the little varmints." So, Mimi reluctantly handed the kids the sandwiches she had packed in four neat paper sacks and watched the kids excitedly trudge between the cars to the back car of the train.

The kids tossed their carry-ons and the sandwich bags onto an extra seat, then took their own seats facing one another–two boys and two girls. The car was almost empty, which was good, Christina thought. They could talk freely and maybe not get fussed at for talking too loud.

But as the train roared to life, the steam building in its belly, and began its *c h u g, c h u g, chug,*

chugchugchug along the track, the kids were too excited to speak. They each mashed their nose–piggy style– against the frosty window. With each clackety-clack along the rail track, they left the town of Durango behind. Then, with a giant gasp of steam and the blowing of a horn that sounded like *WHOOOOOOOOOOOOOOOOOOOOOO!* the train headed up through the mountains toward the little town of Silverton.

They couldn't believe the scenery. The feel. The sound. It was like being in a movie, or at least like one of those movie theme parks. It was fun. It was scary. It was thrilling. It was noisy. And it was cold.

"What a ride!" Christina trilled. She wiped frosty fog from the window and looked out at the beautiful snowscape.

"We're climbing, that's for sure!" said Zander. Indeed, they seemed to be headed for the sky.

"Here's one of those cliffs Mimi talked about," Dakota said. She had a slight tremble in her voice. And didn't they all, as the train lurched left and right around a hairpin turn–and all you could see out the window was nothingness. The train seemed to cling to the side of the mountain like a very brave mountain goat.

"Railroad bridge coming up!" Grant called.

"Ohhhhhh," said Dakota. "No wonder Mimi said what she did. I'll bet Papa's laughing now."

But the kids didn't laugh. They just sat stock still and watched as the train took them across a frozen abyss. It was a lot like flying in Papa's little airplane, Christina thought.

The door to their train car popped open and the conductor paraded inside. "You kids having fun?" he asked.

"We sure are," Christina volunteered for all of them. "You must never get tired of this," she added.

The conductor just chuckled. "Uh, sure," he said. "Hey, I've got some cider steaming on the firebox. Want to join me for a warm drink?"

"Sure!" the kids said, eager to get a look at more of the train.

The conductor led them to the next car. While the train's whistle continued to shriek, he poured them mugs of warm apple cider, then stuck a cinnamon stick in each mug for them to stir the dollop of whipped cream he squirted on top. As they sipped the spicy beverage, he told them:

"We're passing through the San Juan National Forest. More than $300 million in gold and silver were hauled on narrow-gauge railroad tracks like this back in the

days of mining. There were a lot of little railroads like this stringing the Rocky Mountains together."

Suddenly, Christina had a thought. "Have you seen a couple of unusual men on the train today?" she asked, much to the surprise of the rest of the kids.

The conductor pulled thoughtfully on his whiskers. His cap was tilted slightly on his head. "Nope. Sometimes you see some folks who like to ride the train dressed like the olden days, so I can't tell one character from another, frankly."

When the conductor glanced at his shiny gold pocket watch, the kids thanked him for the cider. They insisted that they could return to their own car by themselves.

When they got to their car, Grant said, "I'm hungry." He reached for the sandwich sacks, then stopped, his hand outstretched but frozen in place.

"What's wrong?" asked Christina. "Quit horsing around and toss us our lunch."

"Take a look at this," Grant said, not moving.

The kids got up out of their seats and went to look over his shoulder. There on the extra seat, their paper sack lunch bags were lined up neatly. With a thick black marker, someone had written across the bags:

YOUR PAPA DID IT. WE KNOW. WE PLAN TO

HAUNT YOU WHEREVER YOU GO. WHEN WE PICK HIM UP, DON'T BE SURPRISED. YOU'LL HAVE THIS ON YOUR CONSCIENCE ALL YOUR LIVES.

11 Cliff Palace

Christina felt like crying. This was beginning to sound serious. She wanted to tell Mimi and Papa, but what evidence did she really have? Only the kids had seen the men. They hadn't really done anything. Maybe they were just playing a practical joke like she and Grant sometimes did. In fact, that was the problem. Because she and her brother liked to play jokes, Mimi and Papa might not even believe their tale. Mimi had often warned them about the boy who cried, "Wolf!" so often that when a real wolf showed up everyone ignored him. Much to their detriment!

"What do we do now?" asked Zander.

Christina was angry. She thought you should be able to ride a train without being harassed. "We're going to eat our lunch," she said.

Everyone's lunch was the same–peanut butter and jelly sandwich, bag of chips, apple, and brownie, plus two cartons of milk, a straw, and a napkin. Grant immediately opened his chips and put them inside his sandwich. When Zander and Dakota looked at him like he was crazy, Christina said, "He always does that. He usually adds baloney, too."

By the time they finished their late lunch, the clackety-clack sound of the swaying train put them to sleep. Even the wail of the whistle did not awaken them.

Papa had told them this was a special trip of the train. It did not usually go this time of year, that's why it was not so crowded. Only a few special people like Mimi, to do research, had been invited. They were going to spend the night in Silverton and take the train back to Durango early the next morning.

It was dark when Mimi, Papa, the conductor, and two other "helpful" men in a black coat and cap, hauled the kids off the train and into a quaint Victorian bed and breakfast across the street from the depot. The two-story house was decorated in lots of fancy white woodwork called "gingerbread" and was festooned with twinkling white lights.

Christina only got a brief glimpse of the house as

she rode over Papa's shoulder inside the front door to the parlor. With hardly a stir, the kids were tucked into snug bunkbeds in a downstairs room. All night, Christina could have sworn that the beds shifted left and right and creaked and groaned, and that the wind was really the *WHOOOOOOOOOO* of the train whistle.

The next morning, they took the train back to Durango, got their car, and headed off "lickety-split!" Mimi insisted. "We've go to get to Breckenridge by Saturday night and we have one more stop to make," she said.

"I know, I know," said Papa, speeding up. He slipped and slid on the icy street, making the kids squeal with fake fear and delight. Papa had grown up in the Midwest, and so he knew how to drive in winter weather.

As they sped across the state to the west, Mimi told them all some interesting history about the famous Anasazi Indians, today often called the Ancient Ones. Even though, as Mimi explained, Anasazi was actually an Indian word that meant "enemy ancestors."

"The Anasazi culture started here way back when we went from dating time from B.C. to A.D.," Mimi said.

"Or BCE or CE," Christina added, since that was the

term they used in school. "Before the Common Era or the Common Era."

"That's right," Mimi agreed. "Either way, it was a very long time ago."

"Longer ago than the dinosaurs?" asked Grant. He loved dinosaurs.

"No," interjected Zander. "Dinosaurs would have been millions of years ago. I think your grandmother means thousands of years ago."

"Exactly," Mimi agreed once more, then continued. "The first group of Anasazi were known as the Basketmakers. They survived by eating desert plants, hunting animals with spears, and making baskets."

"Did they eat cactus?" Grant asked. He had often had some unfortunate close encounters with cactus spines in his behind!

"Cactus, too," Mimi said and all the kids went "Yuuuuuuuck!" "Over time, they developed bows and arrows, began to make pottery, grew beans and corn, and built underground pit houses. The place we're headed to visit–Cliff Palace at Mesa Verde National Park–is an example of how their culture evolved."

Christina looked out the car window. It was hard to imagine America before it was the United States. Then the

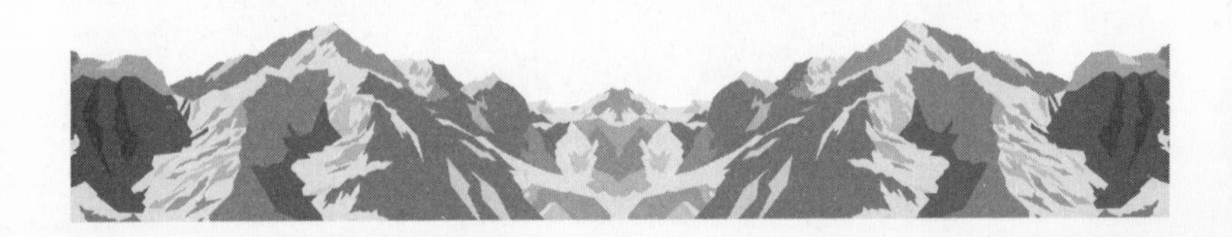

Nothing like a road trip!

land had belonged to the native peoples. When outsiders came, whether from England or Spain or anyplace else, they pretty much took over the land and killed the Indians (who had no immunity against white man diseases like measles or smallpox) or herded them onto reservations.

"As you can imagine," Mimi went on, "the first non-native people to come to this area and see all these cliff dwellings the Anasazi had left behind were pretty startled to discover that civilization had been here before them."

As Mimi continued her story, they drove across a mesa through a piñon pine forest. The children gasped when they first caught sight of the amazing stone city carved into the mountainside.

"Wow!" said Grant. This is a Cliff Palace."

"It looks like little stone condos–hundreds of them," Christina remarked.

"Look at the stone towers!" Dakota shouted.

"And there are 23 underground ceremonial kivas," Papa said.

"What's a kiva?" asked Zander, gaping up at the stunning scene.

"A kiva is place like a room where the people held their religious ceremonies, right Mimi?" Christina said. "I think we learned that way back in kindergarten."

"That's right," said Mimi. "And only the Pueblo people could attend. It was very private."

Grant pointed toward a ladder that looked like it would take you down into a kiva. "Then why are those guys going down there?"

Christina gasped. It was the dumb old Trenchcoat Tommyknockers, as she had begun to call them in her head. They'd been followed again. She had no idea how they were keeping up with them on such a long trip.

The rest of the kids were too busy exploring to worry about the men.

"Don't pick up any rocks!" Mimi warned them. "It's against the law. This place is an archaeological treasure you know. If everyone took even a little piece of rock away with them as a souvenir, this place would soon look like a desert."

"Shucks," said Grant, pulling a red rock out of his pocket and tossing it on the ground–*kerplunk.*

And then, not surprisingly, each of the other kids went:

Klunk,
Thunk,
Blunk
as they tossed their souvenir rocks on the ground.

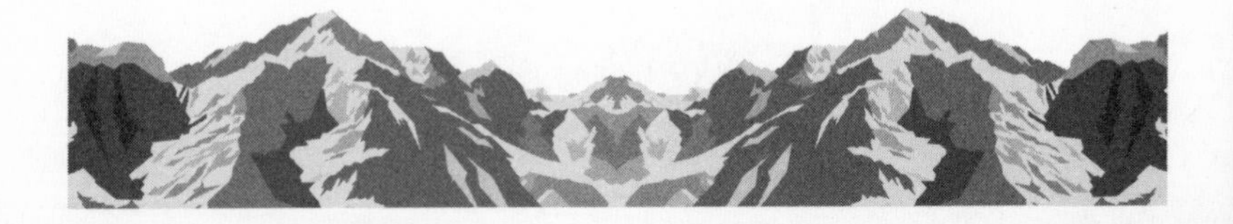

Soon, they all spread out in different directions. Christina headed toward the kiva where the men were just climbing out. She noted that one man was very tall and the other very short, sort of like Mutt and Jeff, she thought. In spite of her efforts to catch up with them, they were too far away. And anyway, Mimi called that it was time to go.

"But I could stay here forever!" Zander said. "It's a really neat place. Lots of exploring to do."

"It seems very mysterious to me," said Christina. "I would not want to be out here in the dark all by myself."

"Well you will be if you don't get in this vehicle," Papa teased. And again, even as they loaded the car, no one noticed the pink puddles of light the red flasher beneath the car *beeped beeped beeped* out.

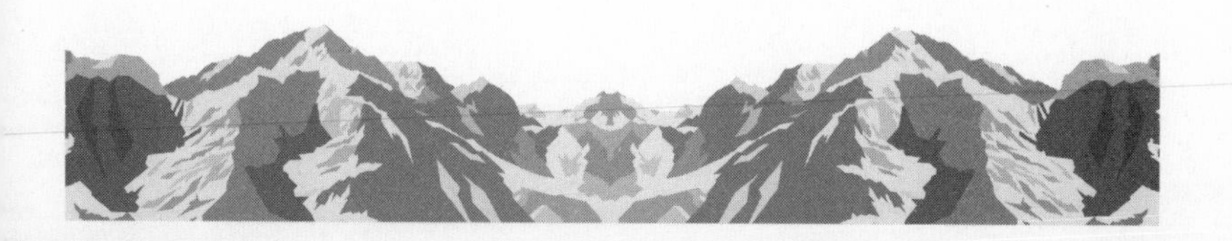

12 Back to Breckenridge

As they drove back across the desert, Papa sang old cowboy songs like "I'm an old cowhand, from the Rio Grande," and "Oh, give me a home where the buffalo roam."

The kids sang along, then stared out the window until they grew bored even with the beautiful scenery. Slowly, one by one, they put on headphones and listened to music, or read in their new books, snacked on the Snakesnack Mix Mimi had made, or dozed off to dream of life hundreds of years ago in the Rocky Mountains.

Later, they played a game, trying to name dinosaurs by their real Latin names in alphabetical order.

"Allosaurus," said Grant. And when everyone else was stumped, he added, "Apatosaurus."

"Brontosaurus!" Dakota squealed.

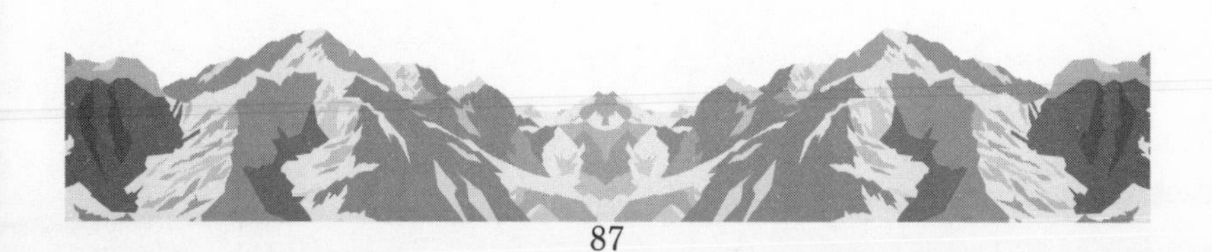

"Ceratosaurus," said Zander.

"Is that a real dino?" Mimi asked, and Zander promised it really was.

Finally Christina spoke up. "Dryosaurus."

"Now that can't be real!" Papa argued. "What is that? A dino that's having a bad hair day, or something?"

The kids laughed, but Grant pulled out the dino pocket guide he kept in his backpack and looked it up. "Dryosaurus," he said. "It's the real thing." The other kids groaned.

"Well, I'm Thirstyosaurus," Christina said. "Can we stop and get something to drink?"

"Suuuuuure!" Mimi said, waving her hand out the window.

The kids looked out and saw a vast expanse of nothingness. Just plains and mountains and sky. Christina peered at the rear view mirror to see if there was anything promising they had recently passed. In the distance she spied a small black dot. She knew in her heart that it was the black sedan.

"Someone's following us," Christina said. Everyone just laughed and continued their dinosaur game. Mimi handed out foil pouches of lemonade, and the only sound in the car for the next mile was *sluuuuuuuuuurp*.

It was after midnight when they came through the last mountain pass and arrived in the old mining town of Breckenridge. Everyone was asleep except Christina. She was settled deep into the seat and plaid blanket. Silently she watched out the window as the deserted town came into view.

Papa drove slowly down the Main Street which was decorated with thousands of twinkly white lights. It was like a little Swiss village, Christina thought. All the little gingerbready houses and gaily decorated shops glistening in snow seemed right out of a Hans Christian Andersen fairy tale.

Behind the town was spread a long range of mountain peaks. Lights lit up a crisscross of wide ski trails. An enormous spray of sparkling snow spewed from the jets of the snow-making equipment. A snowcat crawled across the trails, grooming them.

At the top of the hill, Papa turned the SUV into a snowy driveway. *"Crunnnnch"* went the tires as they made a path into a parking space. Christina looked at the sign perched in front of the most beautiful log house she had ever seen. The sign read: Allaire Timbers Inn.

Christina knew that this was the inn that Mimi's and Papa's friends ran. Two little groves of decorated Christmas trees swayed in the wind. Moonlight glistened on the snow-covered roof. If Santa had flown in and plunked right down by the chimney, Christina thought it would not have surprised her at all!

Mimi helped Christina get out of the car and they stepped gingerly over the snow until they got to the porch. Mimi lifted up the paw of a wooden bear and found the door key the innkeepers had left for their late arrival. As quietly as she could, Mimi opened the door and Christina dove into the large living room where a fire was still crackling in the fireplace. Everything was decorated for Christmas. It was beautiful, and best of all the whole place smelled like cinnamon and ginger and apples and peppermint.

Christina spied a large cookie jar and a big pitcher of milk on the sideboard. Before she could investigate, someone behind her thrust a handful of snow down the back of her shirt. "Yiiii!" Christina squealed. She turned to see Zander standing there with a grin on his face. Behind him was Dakota, rubbing her eyes, looking around like she was lost. Papa followed behind with luggage in one hand and a sleeping Grant

tossed over his shoulder.

"Shhhhh!" Mimi warned them all. "Guests are asleep." She handed Christina a key. "You girls are in the Bear Pass room," she said, nodding toward a log staircase that led upstairs. "Grab your stuff and get to bed." She blew kisses to the girls, then turned to help Papa.

Neither Christina nor Dakota argued. They tugged their backpacks up the carpeted stairs, trying to be as quiet as possible. After they got in the room, Christina slipped back out and padded back down the stairs. The big room was empty. She went to the sideboard and got two large cookies from the jar and put them on a paper plate. Then she poured a big glass of milk and turned to go upstairs.

Perhaps it was just her imagination, but outdoors in the darkness, Christina thought she saw a face in the window. Surely it was just a glare or reflection, she thought. In spite of standing near the fire, she shivered as goosebumps popped up on her forearms and across the back of her neck.

It can't be them, she said to herself. We've driven so far and so long; surely those nasty men have lost us by now. Besides, those two thugs wouldn't be

allowed to stay in this nice inn. When an ember popped behind her, Christina jumped, almost dropping the cookies and spilling the milk.

"I'm going to bed," she said aloud. "So there!" And she climbed the stairs and did just that.

13 Allaire "Timber!"'s Inn

The next morning, Christina and Dakota awoke to discover themselves in a room filled with teddy bears!

"I guess it's because it's the Bear Pass room," Dakota speculated.

"Mimi said each room is named after a famous mountain pass," Christina told her. "I'm glad we got this room."

Dakota licked the sparkly crumbs off her lips. "I'm glad you got the cookies and milk last night."

"Me, too!" said Christina, gulping down the last bite of her cookie. She felt great after getting a good night's sleep in the big bed with the warm quilts and coverlets on it. When she raised the mini-blind at the window, the two girls were surprised to see all the bright sunshine.

"Wow! Are we going up there?" Dakota asked,

pointing to the ski slopes in the distance.

"I sure hope so!" said Christina.

Suddenly their door burst open. There stood Grant and Zander already decked out in ski suits. "Anybody going skiing?!" Grant cried.

"Hey, don't leave without us," Christina begged.

"We're not," said Zander. "We're just headed downstairs for breakfast. And by the way, could you take that ski pole out of my eye?" he teased Grant.

"Oops, sorry," said Grant. He had his hands full with skis, poles, hat, scarf, and mittens.

"Hey, Grant, what's all that stuff sticking out of your ski suit?" Dakota asked with a giggle.

Grant looked down at his ankles and sighed. "Oh, it's just my long johns. They're longer than my ski suit and so they stick out."

When the girls began to laugh uncontrollably, Zander led Grant away. "They can't help it, Grant," he reassured his cousin. "They've got teddy bear brains."

Downstairs, every table except one was filled with guests eating breakfast and talking like they were old friends.

Are these poles too big?

"Do you know these people?" Christina asked Mimi.

"No," said Mimi. "But that's part of the fun of staying at a bed and breakfast inn–you get to meet a lot of new friends."

The four kids plopped down at the empty table and were soon served hot flapjacks. "Just like the gold miners used to eat!" promised the innkeeper. They also had orange juice smoothies. Since they didn't remember ever having dinner, they discovered that they were famished. They ate all their breakfast and asked for seconds.

"Carbing up for the slopes?" a man at the next table asked them.

"Yep!" said Grant, then turned to his sister and whispered, "What's that mean?"

"It means you're going to need all the energy you can get today!" said Papa. "We're going to ski awhile, then take a snowmobile ride up to the Continental Divide, and then if you're not exhausted, we're going to go ice skating."

When everyone around them laughed, Mimi came over and said to Papa, "Pick one! Remember, we are going to the Ski Ball tonight." That made the girls smile and the guys groan. But not Papa–he loved to dance. "I'm going to stay here by the fire and read and write."

"Well, I'll put it to a vote," he told the kids. "What

do you want to do?"

All four kids voted to "Ski!!!!!!" and soon they got all their thick layers of clothing on and headed toward the door.

"Wait!" said Grant.

"What is it?" Papa asked impatiently. It was really warm in the room with the roaring fire with all those clothes on.

"I gotta go!" Grant insisted.

"Then GO!" Papa grumbled.

Grant ran off, tossing clothes left and right, as the others headed on out to the snow-covered car. By the time they scraped the ice off the windows and got inside, Grant reappeared with his clothes mostly back on.

"Let's hit the slopes!" said Papa.

None of the kids had been skiing before, but that did not bother them. First they had to get their passes put on their jackets, then stand in line at the ski lift.

"What do we do?" Christina asked Papa for the third time. She was getting nervous.

"Just stand like this," said Papa. "And when the chair gets to you, sit down. Then when you get to the top,

get off. It's easy."

As soon as he said this, he and Grant and Zander boarded the chair lift and disappeared with a backwards wave.

Christina and Dakota held onto one another. The lift operator slowed the chair down when it came to them and they sat down. Once they were on, he let the chair go and up they swooped into the sky.

At first it was scary, then it was fun. "I really like this!" Christina said. She gazed out over the slopes and the tops of the trees covered with snow.

"I just hope we can get off," Dakota said nervously.

"Well, if we have to, we'll just fall off!" Christina teased.

But at the top of the mountain, that's exactly what they did! Even though Papa had warned the operator to slow the chair lift down, the girls both tangled their crossed skis and fell–SPLAT!–face first into the soft, powdery snow. The man held the chair until the girls managed to get up and get out of the way.

"Well, that was certainly embarrassing," Christina grumbled. Papa came over and brushed the snow from her bangs. "It's ok," he said. "That's the only way to learn. You didn't hear anyone laughing, did you?"

"No," said Dakota. "Why not? We must have looked pretty stupid."

Papa laughed. "No one laughed because everyone out here has fallen plenty of times. It's called SKIING!"

"We got off the chair lift right," Grant bragged.

Papa laughed again. "That's because I picked you two guys up by the scruff of your necks and plunked you off!"

Zander laughed so hard that his skis slid out from under him and tapped Grant's skis and they both fell down.

"Timber!" Grant cried.

"Real cool, dudes," said Christina with a smug little smile.

As they inched their way to the hilltop, Christina looked out over the beautiful view. She could see mountains all around. Gigantic fir trees towered over them. One limb let go of a handful of snow which fell down upon them like glittery fairy dust. Down below, the town of Breckenridge looked like the miniature Christmas village Mimi put on the mantle each year.

"What now?" Zander asked.

"There are several slopes we can go down," Papa

said. "You want to stay on the green 'bunny' slopes," he warned. "You definitely don't want to go down a slope marked with a black diamond. If we get separated, we'll meet at the bottom at the Skihaus."

Grant misunderstood. "There's a skiing horse at the bottom?"

"No," said Papa. "The Skihaus is the restaurant. Now everyone follow me!"

Slowly, Papa started off, his skis carving an S-shape in the snow. Zander followed, using his poles to help him manage the turns. Grant followed. His knees were bent and his backside jutted out, but he was keeping up.

The girls edged nearer and nearer to the top of the hill where they would start down. Just as they were about to go over the top, a rude snowboarder swept by them and caused them both to slide toward a different slope. This slope had a black diamond marking it. Before they could stop themselves with a "snowplow" move, they involuntarily started down the steep slope.

Papa looked back just in time to see them. "See you at the bottom!" he cried, unable to turn around and get back up the hill. "Be carefullllllllll!"

At first it wasn't too bad. Giggling nervously, the two girls held tightly to their ski poles and inched down the

slope. But as the slope grew steeper, they went faster in spite of anything they could do.

Suddenly, the slope flattened out a little and the skiing became fun and easier. But then, they came around a turn and up and over a mogul hill, and then–swoooooooosh! A steep incline seemed to suck them down the mountain

"Yiiiiiiiii!" screamed Christina.

"Arrrrrrrr!" cried Dakota.

Christina didn't know if the tears in her eyes were from the stinging cold or from fear, or both. All she knew is that there was no one on this slope to help them. They were dashing faster and faster down the mountain, and the edge of the cliffs looked scarily close.

Then things got worse. On the shady side of the mountain, the snow had frozen to ice. Now they scooted even faster down the mountain. Christina had no idea how they were even staying on their skis. And then suddenly, they weren't!

KERPLUMMMMMMPF! That was Christina, plowing headfirst into a giant snowdrift on the side of the slope.

PLUMPH! PLUMPH! PLUMPH! That was Dakota, scooting feet first into a snowbank on the other

side of the slope.

And then, there was silence. The only sound was gently shifting snow and a soft whimper.

Christina picked her face up out of the snow. She looked like a snowman. "Are you ok?" she called to Dakota.

Dakota took a deep breath. "I think I'm alive," she said. "But I don't think I can get up."

"Me either," Christina admitted. The thick powdery snow practically had her buried.

Suddenly, there was a double swoosh behind them. The girls looked up, hoping to see Papa or the ski patrol with their snowmobile. Instead, two dark figures hovered over them. The tails of their black trenchcoats were rimmed with snow; their black caps topped by a white mound of snow.

"Need help, girlies?" the first man said. Without waiting for an answer, he grabbed Christina up out of the snowdrift and tucked her under one arm.

With a grunt, the second man did the same to Dakota.

The two girls stared at one another in fear. They couldn't speak. And then, the two men took off down the slope, girls in tow, zigging and zagging left and right down the curves. Christina pressed her eyes shut tightly. She

couldn't bear to look. What were they going to do to them? Throw them off the mountain? Kidnap them?

Just when her imagination had run away with her even more wildly than the skiers had, she felt the man release her. The other man did the same to Dakota. The two men sped off down another slope marked with two black diamonds. But they had left the girls at the top of a tiny hill that went right to the steps of the Skihaus.

Holding hands tightly, Christina and Dakota–their knees quivering like Jell-O®–managed to slide to the steps and fall down on them.

"Let's get this stuff off," Christina said. She and Dakota took off their skis and poles and stood them on a metal stand. They brushed the snow from their clothes and shook out and straightened their hats. Then they went inside. Dakota sat at a log table to watch for the others. Christina fished in her pocket for some change and got in line. When it was her turn, she said to the waitress, "Ttttwwwo hhhot cchhoocolates, ppplease."

14 The Ski Ball

Later that afternoon, back at the inn, the four kids put on their bathing suits and climbed into the steaming, bubbling hot tub on the deck. They wore their dried off ski caps because it was snowing.

They each stuck their tongues out to catch the icy flakes.

"I am sooooo sore," Zander admitted. "I must have skied a hundred miles."

"I'm not sore," bragged Grant. "I never even fell down."

Zander looked at Christina and Dakota who were both uncommonly quiet. "Hey, where did you two go? We looked for you on the slopes. When we finally found you at the Skihaus, you both looked whupped."

The two girls looked at one another. But in spite

of wanting to relay their adventure, they just couldn't. Finally Christina managed to peep, "We just skied." Then she and Dakota startled the boys by bursting into laughter, then slipping beneath the water, hats and all!

The annual Ski Ball, which was a benefit for the local kids who were training to try to get in the Olympics one day, was quite an affair!

At the inn, all the guests had oohed and aahed over Mimi's swanky black dress and hot pink dancing shoes. Christina wore a white dress with a red and green sash that Mimi had made for her; she loved it because it made her feel beautiful and so grown up. Dakota had brought some dressy jeans covered in rhinestones to wear with a frilly blouse and cool vest; she even wore a cute cowboy hat with rhinestones on the band.

Papa looked movie star handsome in his tuxedo–what he joked was his "penguin get-up." Grant and Zander wore tuxedoes too, and looked perfectly miserable.

"What's this thing around my waist?" Grant had grumbled.

"It's a cummerbund," Papa informed him.

"Well, it feels like a cumbersomebund to me," groused Grant.

Secretly, the girls thought the boys looked great–but they would never tell them!

It snowed all the way to the Ski Ball which was held in a large glassed-in conference center. Fortunately, there was Papa's favorite–valet parking–so they could dash inside and get warm quickly.

"Wow!" Christina said with a gasp. "Look at this place!"

The Ball theme was "Snows of Long Ago" and every corner was decorated with enormous fake fir trees dripping with cotton snow. They looked entirely real. There were gigantic photographs of people from the past dressed in old-timey winter clothes. Some held funny-looking skis that were much taller than they were, or stood on clunky-looking snowshoes.

Mimi sighed as she looked at the photos. "The more things change, the more they stay the same."

"What does that mean, Mimi?" Christina asked, confused.

Mimi patted her shoulder. "See all these families

in the snow, trying to stay warm, having fun, acting silly? Well haven't we been doing the same thing?"

"Yeah, except fortunately we have modern equipment!" said Grant. "Look how they had to get up the ski slopes–holding on to a rope while it towed them up the mountain. I'll take a chair lift anyday."

"Not me," muttered Dakota under her breath, and Christina giggled.

"What's so funny?" Grant demanded.

"I think Mimi means that we could come back here in 100 years and you'd see new photos, only people would be wearing space-age ski suits and probably have rocket-propelled skis. But they'd still be families having fun. Like a tradition. Right, Mimi?"

Mimi smiled at all the children. "Something like that," she agreed.

"Let's eat!" said Papa, and they all followed him into a large banquet hall where amazing ice sculptures on tables depicted the Rocky Mountains. The holiday-decorated tables were laden with mounds of fresh shrimp, cheese and crackers, fruit, and bowls of nuts.

Mimi and Papa helped themselves to the hors d'oeuvres, and went off to visit with friends.

The kids nibbled a little then wandered over to the

silent auction going on in another room.

"What? We can't talk?" asked Grant. "What kind of party is this?"

"No," said Christina. "Look around. The *silent* means you bid on auction items by writing your name and the amount you will pay on the sheets of paper on the clip boards beside every item up for auction. At the end of the auction, the highest bidder wins. The items have been donated. All the money goes to benefit the ski program."

"Hmmmmm," said Grant, looking around carefully at the incredible array of stuff. Sure, there were paintings, and vases, and jewelry, and clothes . . . but there were tables of cool sporting goods and toys and games, and even stuffed animals. "Guess I'll place a bid or two," he said and headed off.

"You'd better not!" Christina warned him. "You have to pay real money if you win. You'd better go ask Mimi and Papa."

Grant just continued to saunter off like a big-shot. "Oh, they won't care," he called back over his shoulder. "Besides, I have my allowance in my pocket."

"Well, I tried," Christina said disgustedly. But she admired Grant's gumption to give something new a shot.

The other three kids went and stood in front of a gigantic video screen that was showing snippets of events that the Olympic-wanta-be kids had participated in the last year. They were skiing downhill at what looked like the speed of light. They were zipping through the pipeline of hard-packed snow on their snowboards doing fancy jumps. And they were ice skating like the professionals on TV.

"Wow!" said Zander. "I wish I lived out here. Wouldn't it be fun to do all those cool things all winter?"

"It would be cool, that's for sure," Grant agreed. "But think about where we live. We get to go to the beach and surf and stuff like that."

"When I grow up, I'm going to have a summer house at the beach and a winter house in the mountains," said Christina.

Soon, they all went into dinner and joined Mimi and Papa at a big round table just for them that was decorated with green pine, red candles, and glitter all over the white tablecloth. The ballroom had a large wooden dance floor topped by a ceiling full of red, white, and green balloons in a big net. A band was playing at

one end of the dance floor.

Mimi and Papa did not even think about eating. They headed for the dance floor.

"Hey, let's dance, too!" Christina said.

"No way," said Zander.

"I love to dance!" said Grant and led the way, wiggling through other round tables right to the center of the dance floor. Dakota followed eagerly; Zander reluctantly trudged along behind.

On the dance floor, Grant didn't even need a partner. He just went right into his wild and crazy dance style that everyone loved. Pretty soon, adults dancing nearby stopped and watched Grant. They began to clap their hands in tune to the music. That just egged Grant on, and he soon became a whirling dervish. The other kids laughed and clapped too. When the music stopped, everyone applauded Grant, who took a big bow. His bow tie was crooked and his cummerbund was dangling behind him like a beavertail, but he had a big grin on his face.

When the music began again, it was a slow dance, and the kids headed back to the table for ice water. Two waiters immediately appeared to fill their glasses. Christina looked up to say thank you and frowned. It was

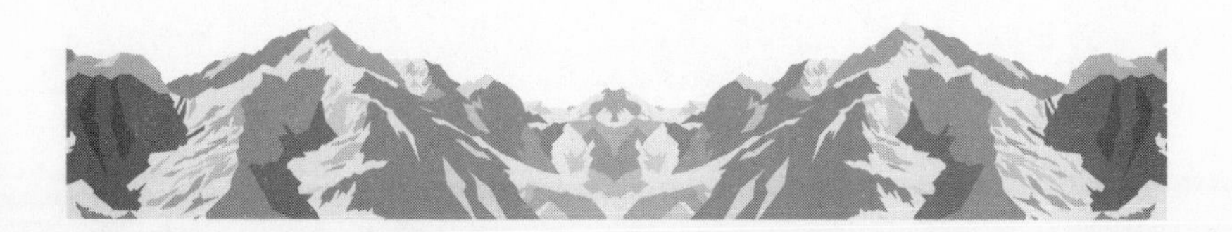

the two guys. They wore waiter outfits, but she recognized them.

"You guys had better leave us alone!" she said to the short Mutt man.

"I have no idea what you're talking about," he said prissily.

"Oh, yes you do," Christina barked. "You've been following us and I don't know why. My Papa hasn't done anything. But he's on the dance floor and when he comes back, I'm going to get him to run you two right out of here. I think it's against the law to follow people around. You two could go to jail."

"Hey," said the tall Jeff man, menacingly. "Your Papa is the one who's up to illegal things. He'll go to jail. You just wait and see. Besides, didn't we help you up off the ski slope?"

Christina grinned. "I thought you didn't have any idea what I was talking about? I'm going to find a police officer." When Christina started to get up, the two men scooted off, weaving between the tables, and disappeared out the ballroom door.

"I think they'll leave us alone now," Christina told the other kids, but they looked doubtful.

When the dinner and dancing were done, the master of ceremonies announced the winners in the silent auction.

"I didn't bid," said Mimi.

"Me either," said Papa. "We might as well go."

"GRANT YOTHER!" called the announcer suddenly. Everyone in the room turned to look at Grant who looked down at his desert plate.

"Graaaant?" said Mimi.

"Granttttttttttttttt!" said Papa.

Grant looked up sheepishly. "Well, I think I just bought my Christmas presents?"

They couldn't help it–they all laughed. Especially when someone let the net loose and all the balloons snowed down upon the guests.

Mimi and the girls went to get their coats while Papa and the boys went to find out what Grant had "won" in the silent auction. Christina was pretty sure it would cost a lot more than Grant's puny allowance.

At the front door, the valet appeared with their SUV. It was dark and cold and snowy. As they put Grant's gifts in the car and got in themselves, the valet asked Papa to come to the back of the car. Soon, Papa

returned. He was very angry. He held a red flashing box in his hand.

"Now just what do you suppose this is?" he asked Mimi. "The valet noticed it beneath our car. He said he thought it was some kind of tracking device. Now why would our rental car have such a thing?"

Mimi was upset too. "Maybe it's a mistake?"

There was a lot of rustling and punching and loud whispers of "Christina" . . ."Christina" . . .in the back seat.

Papa jerked around. "You kids don't know anything about this do you?" he demanded.

"Well," began Christina, knowing she should confess. "Not really, but since Denver two weird guys have been following us. They seem harmless. They even helped me and Dakota on the ski slope. But they think you did something bad, Papa, and say they will take you to jail."

Mimi and Papa stared at one another with big eyes. Then together, they said the same thing: "SINCE DENVER?!?!?!?!"

"Why didn't you tell us?" Mimi asked.

"We didn't want there to be a mystery on our vacation," Christina said. "We thought they would just go

away. I didn't know they had a tracking thing on our car."

"You should always tell," Mimi said gently. "Adults are always here to help. Maybe these guys are dangerous!"

They were all silent. Only the crunch of snow beneath the tires was heard as Papa drove off into the night and back to the inn.

"Aren't you going to tell that you saw the guys at the ball?" Zander whispered to Christina.

"Aren't we in enough trouble?" she whispered back.

15 The Eisenhower Tunnel

The next day, they packed up and left. It was time to head back to Denver. Everyone was still pretty quiet. Mimi and Papa weren't angry, but they were worried about the two strange men and all the talk about Papa and jail. But with the tracking device off the car, Christina knew the matter was over. She was sad to think that their winter vacation was over so soon.

Pretty soon, Mimi and Papa were in a good mood and telling them more Rocky Mountain history as they drove down the interstate highway.

"In a minute, we'll be going through the Eisenhower Tunnel," Papa said. "It cuts beneath the mountains right under the Continental Divide. It's quite an engineering marvel."

"What's the Continental Divide?" Dakota asked.

"It's the point of the highest mountain ranges in the West," said Papa. "The rivers on one side flow to the east; on the other side they flow to the west."

As they zoomed into the tunnel, the kids squealed. Papa blew the horn of course. It was so dark he had to turn on the headlights. When they finally zipped out the other side, Christina turned to look behind them. She couldn't believe what she saw! This time, she was telling!!

"Papa! Those men are behind us. I promise."

"How?" said Mimi. "You removed the tracker."

Papa did not speak. He only narrowed his eyes and grimaced. He picked up his cell phone and dialed 911. He said a few words, then pulled off at the Scenic Overlook parking area. As he suspected, the black sedan behind him followed them.

Papa got out of the car. The men got out of their car. Mimi and the kids followed Papa.

"Now just what are you two up to?" Papa asked the men. He was angry, but he was not yelling. Not yet.

"Look, sir," said the tall man. "We are undercover private eyes. We were hired to track this car. It's been involved in a theft ring of new rental vehicles. We were told to track it. We've checked the records. Your name appears on the rental receipt. We are going to arrest you, and we'd

appreciate your cooperation."

Now Papa yelled! "You ignoramuses! This is a rental car. I just rented it. I didn't steal it. Besides, do car thieves usually run around in their stolen cars with a wife and bunch of kids and go skiing and dancing?" It was clear Papa thought that these were the two dumbest men he had ever met.

But the two men didn't back down. One pulled a pair of handcuffs off his belt. The other yanked out a baseball bat. They headed toward Papa. Christina was so scared that she cried out, "No!"

Just then, the patrol car that Papa had called pulled into the parking lot. An officer jumped out. When the two men saw him, they stopped.

"I'll take those!" the officer said. "Tell me your names!"

The two men looked scared. "I'm William Mutterly. He's Bill Jefferson."

The kids burst out laughing. The adults stared at them like they were crazy.

"What in the world is so funny?" asked Papa.

"They really are Mutt and Jeff!" said Christina.

Mimi, Papa, and the officer looked at the two men and they began to grin, then laugh at the short and tall men

who really did look like a Mutt and a Jeff and had the names to match.

Then the officer got serious. "We've had a report on two guys meeting this description," he said. "They go around tracking expensive new SUVs, often rentals, then accuse the driver of stealing it. Then they force the driver into an old car they've stolen, and they steal the new car. But not anymore. Mutterly and Jefferson: you're under arrest!"

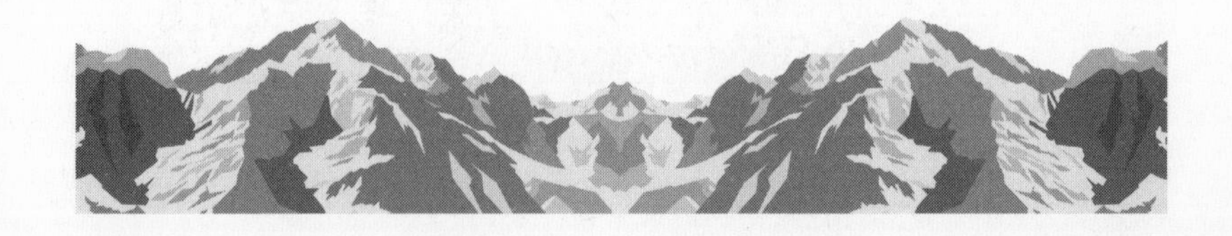

All solved! Let's go ski!!

16 It's Snow Fun

"It's snow fun going home," Grant complained.

Christina giggled. "You said snow instead of no."

"Actually it is snow fun," said Mimi, as Papa pulled the SUV in front of the arrival terminal at the Denver Airport.

"What do you mean?" asked Christina. "I don't understand." She felt grouchy. She didn't want to go home yet either. There was more school vacation left. And now they didn't have those pesky thieves to worry about anymore.

Suddenly, Christina's and Grant's parents and Zander's and Dakota's dad Don appeared on the curb and waved happily. They stood beside an enormous pile of luggage including what looked like skis in a holder.

The kids screamed. "Why are they here? We're not

going home, are we?"

Mimi laughed. "No," she admitted. "This is a last minute surprise. A little serendipity–something fun you weren't expecting, hey?"

"This is GREAT!" said Christina, opening the car door and hugging her mom.

"What are we going to do now?" asked Grant eagerly.

"Take the Ski Train and go to Winter Park to ski," said Mimi.

"Go to Rocky Mountain National Park," said Uncle Don as he hugged his kids.

"Eat chili, lots of chili!" said Dad, trying to stuff his skis in the crowded back.

Only Papa looked troubled. He stared at the car.

"What's wrong?" asked Mimi, worriedly.

Papa motioned to all the people and all the luggage. "I think we're gonna need another SUV," he said.

"Let's just don't get another Mutt and Jeff one," Christina suggested with a giggle.

Christina's Mom looked confused. "What's that mean?"

Mimi and Christina exchanged secretive glances. "Oh, I think we'll just keep that little Christmas mystery to

ourselves," Mimi said.

"Sort of like a Silent Auction?" said Grant.

"Very silent," Christina agreed. *"Very silent!"*

The End

ABOUT THE AUTHOR

Carole Marsh is an author and publisher who has written many works of fiction and non-fiction for young readers. She travels throughout the United States and around the world to research her books. In 1979 Carole Marsh was named Communicator of the Year for her corporate communications work with major national and international corporations.

Marsh is the founder and CEO of Gallopade International, established in 1979. Today, Gallopade International is widely recognized as a leading source of educational materials for every state and many countries. Marsh and Gallopade were recipients of the 2004 Teachers' Choice Award. Marsh has written more than 16 Carole Marsh Mysteries™. Years ago, her children, Michele and Michael, were the original characters in her mystery books. Today, they continue the Carole Marsh Books tradition by working at Gallopade. By adding grandchildren Grant and Christina as new mystery characters, she has continued the tradition for a third generation.

Ms. Marsh welcomes correspondence from her readers. You can e-mail her at carole@gallopade.com, visit the carolemarshmysteries.com website, or write to her in care of Gallopade International, P.O. Box 2779, Peachtree City, Georgia, 30269 USA.

Built-In Book Club
Talk About It!

1. Who was your favorite character? Why?

2. Skiing is a popular sport in Colorado? Why? Can you think of other states where their geography influences what they do for fun?

3. Grant and Christina tried ice skating for the first time in Colorado. Do you like to try new things? How would you feel if you fell down like Grant?

4. If you were one of the kids, would you have been frightened by the message written on the lunch bags? Why or why not?

5. What was the scariest part of the book? Why?

6. If you visited Colorado, what would you most like to do or see?

7. Why were Mimi and Papa upset that the children had not told them someone had been following their car?

8. What was your favorite part of the book? Why?

Built-In Book Club

Bring It To Life!

1. Do a word search! Ask for a volunteer to make a word search with the glossary words in the back of the book. Pass out the puzzle to book club members, and see who finishes first!

2. Map it out! Look at a map of the United States. List the states that Grant and Christina flew over when they traveled from Georgia to Colorado. Then, list the states you would fly over if you traveled from your state to Colorado.

3. Write about it! Write a short newspaper article describing the arrest of the thieves. Be sure to answer the questions who, what, when, where, and why in your story.

4. Are you clueless–or not? Divide the book club into two teams. Direct each team to recall as many clues as they can from the book. List each clue, and then write down how each clue makes sense now that everyone knows the end of the story! The team with the most clues is the winner!

Colorado 'Fourteeners'

There are over 50 'Fourteeners' in Colorado – these are mountain peaks that are over 14,000 feet tall! Here are the top 20 highest 'Fouteeners'!

Peak	*Mtn. Range*	*Elevation*
Mt. Elbert	Sawatch	14,433 ft.
Mt. Massive	Sawatch	14.421 ft.
Mt. Harvard	Sawatch	14,420 ft.
Blanca Peak	Sangre de Christo	14,345 ft.
La Plata Peak	Sawatch	14,336 ft.
Uncompahgre Peak	San Juan	14,309 ft
Crestone Peak	Sangre de Christo	14,294 ft.
Mt. Lincoln	Tenmile-Mosquito	14,286 ft.
Grays Peak	Front Range	14,270 ft.
Mt. Antero	Sawatch	14,269 ft.
Torreys Peak	Front Range	14,267 ft.
Castle Peak	Elk	14,265 ft.
Quandary Peak	Tenmile-Mosquito	14,265 ft.
Mt. Evans	Front Range	14,264 ft.
Longs Peak	Front Range	14,255 ft.
Mt. Wilson	San Juan	14,246 ft.
Mt. Shavano	Sawatch	14,229 ft.
Mt. Belford	Sawatch	14,197 ft.
Crestone Needle	Sangre de Christo	14,197 ft.
Mt. Princeton	Sawatch	14,197 ft.

MEMORABLE MINES

Mining has been a huge part of Colorado history, and is still an important industry today! Check out these memorable Colorado mine names and have a chuckle!

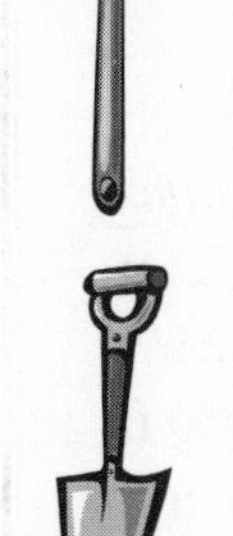
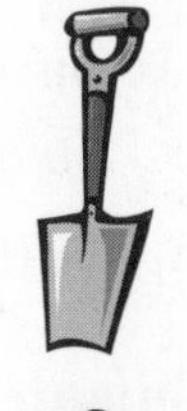

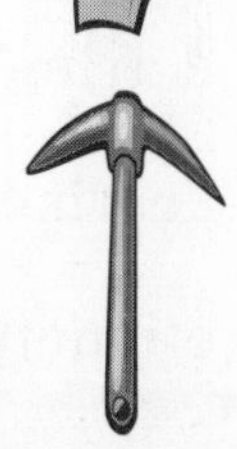

Ace in the Hole Mine
Alice Blue Gown
Anna B Mine
Bacon Strip
Bad Boy Mine
Big Chance Mine
Blue Wrinkle #1
Broken Handle
Buffalo Chip Mine
Chain O' Mines
Chili # 2, 5
Clear Grit Mine
Clinkenbeard
Club Sandwich
Conundrum Mine
Deceiver
Doolittle Mine
Eleven O'Clock Lode
Endomile
Fort Knox Junior
Fortune No. 2 Mine
Four - Most Mine
Go-Boy
Ground Hog Mine
Hardly & Able
Hi - Tension Mine
Hit or Miss
Holy Moses Tunnel
Hot Dog Mine
Humdinger
Lame Duck Shaft
Last Dollar Mine
Little Hope
Lucky Dog
Merry Widow
Midget Mine
Obnoxious
Piddler
Pide Piper
Poopout
Poorman Mine
Prayer #8 & #9
Quandry Tunnel
Teddy Bear Mine
Ten Mile Tunnel
Troublesome Mine
Vacation Mine
We Got Em Mine
Whang Doodle
Why Do Mine
Wimpy
Wolf Tongue Mine
Yo - Jo #15
Zero Mine

It's Snow Much Fun Glossary

alpine: downhill skiing

avalanche: mass of snow that suddenly falls down a mountain, sweeping away or burying everything in its path

big air: term for when a skier or snowboarder comes over a hill and flies through the air before landing on the ground

blizzard: a heavy, blowing snow that often lasts for days, creates large snow drifts, and limits visibility to zero

cross-country: skiing done through a forest or on paths, with no steep hills involved

detriment: a cause of injury or damage

dervish: one who whirls or dances with wild abandonment

etiquette: proper conduct required by society

flatlander: person who lives in a region that's mostly flat

hoodoos: natural and fantastic column of rock in wester North America

moguls: artificially created little hills made for skiers to ski over

sitzmark: name for the indention you leave when you fall bottom-first into the snow

snow angel: made by laying down in the snow with arms and legs extended, then swinging them widely to create "wing" marks in the snow

Snowcat: tractor-like machine with big treads that grooms artificially-blown snow in to a neat pattern

snow cream: ice cream made from snow, sugar, and vanilla flavoring

thundersnow: an unusual weather occurrence when it thunders and lightnings during a snowstorm

vigas: a heavy beam that supports the roof in many forms of southwest Indian and Spanish architecture

warming hut: a primitive shelter where you can stop to get warm or take shelter from bad weather

Scavenger Hunt Quiz!

Recipe for fun: Read the book, and answer the questions below! (Hint: Look high and low!!)

Teachers: you have permission to reproduce this page for your students.

- ❑ 1. Find Denver, Colorado on a map.
- ❑ 2. List 3 kinds of things you might mine for.
- ❑ 3. Draw a Skihaus.
- ❑ 4. How are a ski tow and a chair lift alike?
- ❑ 5. How are a "Mutt" and a "Jeff" different?
- ❑ 6. What do you call a special place where some Native Americans held important ceremonies?
- ❑ 7. Who was the woman who got famous by surviving the sinking of the ocean liner *Titanic*?
- ❑ 8. What powered the Durango-Silverton Narrow Gauge Railroad?
- ❑ 9. What is a silent auction?
- ❑ 10. What does the Continental Divide divide?

The Rocky Mountains

Places To Go & Things To Know!

Denver, Colorado – capital city of Colorado, known as the "Mile High City"

Brown Palace Hotel, Denver, Colorado – historic hotel frequented by many famous guests, including several U.S. presidents

Butterfly Pavilion, Denver, Colorado – indoor tropical rainforest zoo with more than 1,200 exotic butterflies from around the world

Continental Divide, Rocky Mountains – point of the highest mountain ranges in the West

Garden of the Gods, Colorado Springs, Colorado – 480-acre public park, owned by Charles Elliott Perkins of Burlington Railroad, that later was given to the city of Colorado Springs

Colorado Springs, Colorado – founded by General William Jackson Palmer in 1871

Denver, Colorado - capital city of Colorado, known as the "Mile High City"

Brown Palace Hotel, Denver, Colorado - historic hotel frequented by many famous guests, including several U.S. presidents

Butterfly Pavilion, Denver, Colorado - indoor tropical rainforest zoo with more than 1,200 exotic butterflies from around the world

Continental Divide, Rocky Mountains - point of the highest mountain ranges in the West

Garden of the Gods, Colorado Springs, Colorado - 480-acre public park, owned by Charles Elliott Perkins of Burlington Railroad, that later was given to the city of Colorado Springs

Colorado Springs, Colorado - founded by General William Jackson Palmer in 1871
Durango & Silverton Narrow Gauge Railroad, Durango, Colorado - historic railroad, built in 1882, between Durango and Silverton to haul both passengers and mine ores, both gold and silver, from the San Juan Mountains

Rocky Mountain National Park - established in 1915, the park features elevations up to 14,259 feet, 359 miles of trail, 60 peaks for hikers, and Trail Ridge Road (nation's highest, continuous, paved road); visitors can see elk, mule deer, moose, bighorn sheep, black bears, coyotes, cougars, eagles, hawks, fish, and more.

Write Your Own Mystery!

REAL KIDS REAL PLACES

Make up a dramatic title!

You can pick four real kid characters!

Select a real place for the story's setting!

Try writing your first draft!

Edit your first draft!

Read your final draft aloud!

You can add art, photos or illustrations!

Share your book with others and send me a copy!

Six Secret Writing Tips from Carole Marsh!

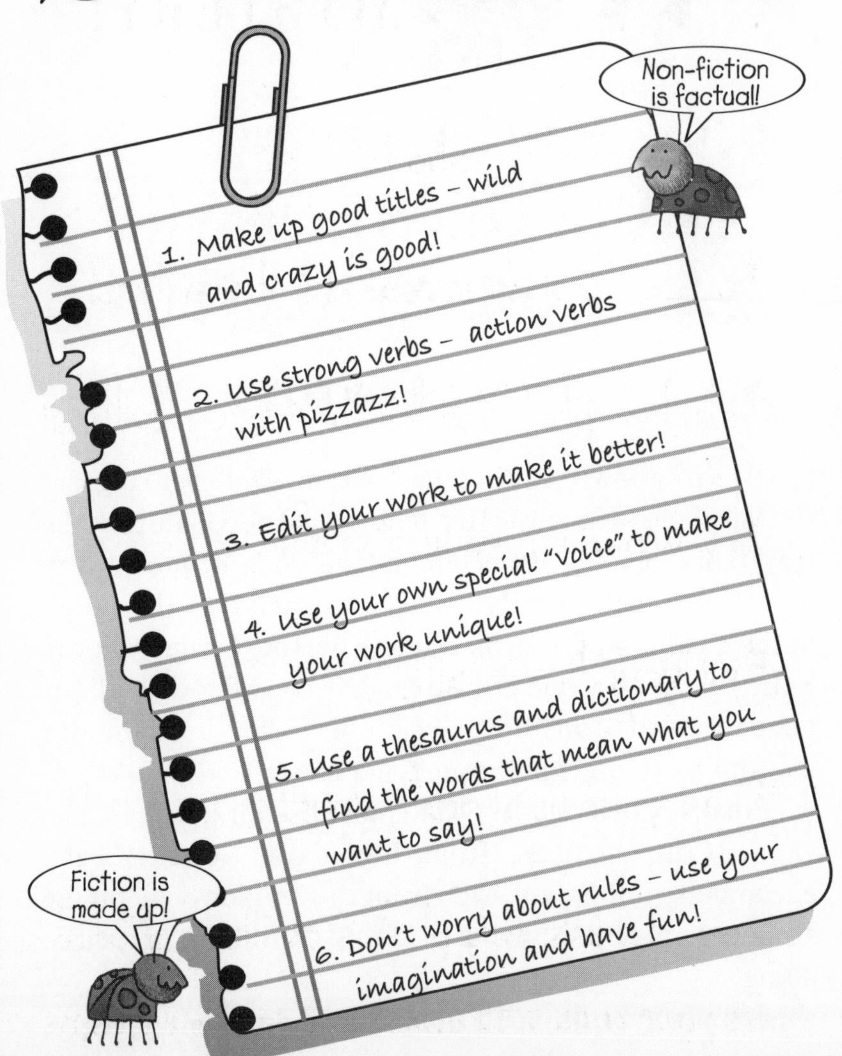

Enjoy this exciting excerpt from

THE GHOST OF THE GRAND CANYON

1 BOUND FOR ADVENURE

"We're almost in Arizona," Grant said, peering out the airplane window. His bouncing knee bumped the tray table causing little lemon-lime soda drops to leap onto Christina's new hot pink cargo pants. She didn't notice. She was too distracted by the Grand Canyon Suite orchestra music blaring from her CD player headset and too busy scanning the horizon for mountains to appear through the haze.

Finally, Christina felt the dampness on her leg. She yanked the headset from her ears. "Grant!" she exclaimed, pulling her eyes from the window and gaping at her soda-dotted pants. "Stop! Watch what you're doing!

Grant's eyes dropped from the window to Christina's

pants. "Uh, oh," he said with a gulp.

"You're ruining my new pants Mimi gave me," Christina whined. "I'm going to be all sticky when this stuff dries...Yuck!"

"I'm sorry!" Grant apologized. "I'm just so excited to see the Grand Canyon, my knee can't keep still. Look, even when I try to hold it down, it just keeps hopping."

Christina swabbed her pants with a napkin, resisting the temptation to, once again, play with the cool zippers on the pockets. The sides of her mouth turned slowly upwards as she noticed Grant's futile attempts to stop his kangaroo-on-coffee knee. He finally gave up and looked helplessly at Christina. They both exploded into laughter.

Suddenly, a loud voice boomed over their heads.

"This is your captain speaking," the man said.

"Hey," Grant said. "It's Captain Speaking. That's the same guy that flew our plane to Alaska."

"Grant," Christina said, trying hard not to laugh at her little brother. "This is the captain speaking, as in...*talking*. That's not his name." Sometimes, Christina thought, experienced nine-year-old big sisters had to cut their younger brothers some slack. After all, it wasn't so long ago that she was seven and not as smart as she was now.

"Ohhhhh," Grant said. Then, in a smaller voice, "Oh." His face reddened as he sneaked glances from side to side to see if anyone else had heard his silly comment.

The pilot's words grabbed their attention. *"We will be touching down in Flagstaff in just a few moments,"* the captain continued. *"The weather is a balmy 110 degrees, but don't worry, with only 10 percent humidity, it's quite pleasant."*

"Pleasant?" Christina said, shooting Grant a disbelieving look. They'd been in hot weather before in their hometown of Peachtree City, Georgia, but 100 degrees was the hottest. Christina remembered it exactly, because that was the day Mimi and Papa filled water balloons and put them in the freezer, just until they got slushy, not frozen solid. Then, they took them outside and the whole family, even Mimi, had a water balloon fight. Christina smiled at the memory. Now, that was a good day, she thought, especially eating the huge bowls of ice cream on the back porch afterwards. Her smile faded as she thought of what 110 degrees felt like–a blasting furnace, she imagined.

"It's 5:22 p.m. Navajo time," the pilot continued. Christina's confusion made deep creases between her brows. Before Mimi had a chance to explain, the pilot's voice returned, *"By the way, Navajo time means one hour be-FORE Arizona time."* He added, *"The Navajo Nation observes daylight savings time, but the rest of the state, including the Hopi Reservation, which is actually surrounded by the Navajo Nation, does not."*

Oh, great, Christina thought. She had a hard enough time keeping her Carole Marsh Mysteries watch set to the right time going from state to state. This was going to be a nightmare. Suddenly, the excitement for her trip to the Grand Canyon was starting to sound not as wonderful as she'd imagined. She usually loved teaming up with Mimi on her adventure trips, but this one was starting to sound a bit more challenging, not to mention sweatier, than any they'd been on before. Mimi always invited Grant and Christina to come along with her on her research trips to get background information for the mystery books she wrote. It seemed every time Grant and Christina accompanied their grandmother, something unexpected happened.

"Mimi?" Grant asked, his voice timid. "What's a Nah-vah-ho?"

"They are the Indians who have lived in the area near the Grand Canyon since the 1400s," Mimi explained.

"Is the lady we're staying with a Navajo Indian?" Christina asked.

"No, actually, she's a Hopi Indian," Mimi reported. "The Hopi have been in Arizona even longer, since the 1100s, believe it or not."

"Wow, that's three hundred years longer than the Navajo and..." Christina was trying to hide her fingers as she counted how many years ago 1100 was from now. She gave up. "That's a really, *really* long time ago," she said to her grandmother.

"About 900 years," Grant said. Christina sighed. Her brother was really good at math.

"I'm looking forward to staying on a real Indian reservation with Nampeyo and her two girls," said Mimi.

"Nam-pay-oh," Grant said, as if saying it more slowly and sounding out each syllable would help him understand its meaning.

"You can call her Nammie," Mimi added. "Evidently, she was named after a famous Indian woman potter and it just so happens she ended up being quite a notable potter, herself."

"I thought you said she was a park ranger, Mimi?" Christina asked.

"Oh, she is," Mimi said. "But she's also become quite well known for her pottery skills."

Grant's nose scooted up his face as though he just ate a whole plate of spinach. He hadn't heard a word after *girl*.

"Wait just a minute," he demanded. "Did you say two girls? TWO *GIRLS*?"

Mimi nodded, "Grant, you'll be fine. Papa's here for male moral support."

"Yeah, but he *likes* girls," Grant said, his shoulders dropping.

"Two girls? That rocks!" Christina beamed. Mimi shot her one of her famous "watch it" looks, then leaned across the aisle and put her hand on Grant's shoulder.

"Listen, buddy, the younger sister is your age. I'm sure you can find something in common," Mimi said.

"Yeah, Grant, we'll *stick* together," Christina reassured him, pointing at her pants with a smile. Grant looked down at the sticky stains and burst out laughing.

The bell sounded indicating it was okay to unbuckle their seatbelts, so Grant and Christina scurried to gather their belongings.

"Yes, kids, we're sure to have fun," Papa said, with a yawn, rousing from his flight-long nap across the aisle. "And who knows what mystery the Valentine State has in store?"

"Valentine State?" Christina repeated his words in a question.

"Yep," Papa said. "Arizona officially became a state on Valentine's Day in 1912. It was the last of the continental states to be given a name, so it's also nicknamed the Baby State," Papa said, smiling at Mimi's impressed expression.

"Hey, I know what it's like to be the baby of the group," said Grant. "I like Arizona much better, definitely."

Christina's mind was still stuck on Papa's mystery comment. She wondered what could possibly be in store for them in a place with thousands of years of Native American history. There was bound to be adventure right around the corner.

CAROLE MARSH MYSTERIES™

WOULD YOU LIKE TO BE A CHARACTER IN A CAROLE MARSH MYSTERY?

If you would like to star in a Carole Marsh Mystery, fill out the form below and write a 25-word paragraph about why you think you would make a good character! Once you're done, ask your mom or dad to send this page to:

Carole Marsh Mysteries Fan Club
Gallopade International
P.O. Box 2779
Peachtree City, GA 30269

My name is: ______________________________

I am a: ____boy ____ girl Age: ______________

I live at: ______________________________

City: ______________ State:____ Zip code: ________

My e-mail address: ______________________________

My phone number is: ______________________________

____

____

____

____

____

____

____

____

____

____

Visit the Carole Marsh Mysteries Website

www.carolemarshmysteries.com

- *Check out what's coming up next! Are we coming to your area with our next book release? Maybe you can have your book signed by the author!*
- *Join the Carole Marsh Mysteries Fan Club!*
- *Apply for the chance to be a character in an upcoming Carole Marsh Mystery!*
- *Learn how to write your own mystery!*